TEN CANDLELIGHT TALES

ff

Ten Candlelight Tales

Alison Uttley

Illustrated by
Irene Hawkins

faber and faber

LONDON · BOSTON

To Janet Elizabeth

First published in 1942
by Faber and Faber Limited
3 Queen Square London WC1N 3AU
Reprinted 1948 and 1952
This paperback edition first published in 1990

Printed in Great Britain by
Richard Clay Ltd Bungay Suffolk
All rights reserved

A CIP record for this book is available from the British Library
ISBN 0-571-14289-3

Contents

The Lion and the Unicorn

George Greensleeve, the son of the farmer at Windy Wood Farm, came home from market one day with a fine young foal. He had bought it for a few pounds from a queer gypsy-looking fellow, a foreigner, with great ear-rings in his ears. Not that the gypsy was anxious to sell it, for he refused surly Tom Dodger's offer of twice the amount, but he seemed to like George's honest face, and he let him have it for a mere song.

It was a good upstanding little foal, with slender legs and strong graceful body and a well-shaped head which it held with pride and dignity as if it were of noble breed. Its coat was white as silver, and although it was rough with lying out, anyone could see it was a thoroughbred. Perhaps it would be a racer, for it trotted up and down when the gypsy spoke to it in his queer lingo, like an Arab steed.

"What a little beauty!" cried Mrs. Greensleeve, holding out a lump of sugar on the palm of her hand. "What will you call it, George?"

"Silver," replied George promptly, patting the foal's neck, and he turned to his wise father and asked his opinion on it.

"There's something amiss, to get it for that price, of course," said Mr. Greensleeve slowly. "What is it, George? Did the fellow tell you?"

"No, I found it out for myself. That's what's the matter." George pointed to the foal's forehead. In the middle of the silky skin was a small lump, no bigger than a pigeon's egg.

"Is that all?" asked Mrs. Greensleeve. "We can soon move that with a little embrocation, poor dear." She stroked the finely arched neck, and the pretty creature turned its head to her and gazed at her with its beautiful dark expressive eyes.

Mr. Greensleeve shook his head as he felt the lump. "Hard as iron," said he. "This won't yield to treatment. Let's hope it won't grow any bigger and be noticeable. It's almost like a calf's horn. Well, we shall see how your Silver goes on."

"He's a grand little horse," said George. "I don't repent buying him. He will repay all we do for him."

He led the little steed to a loose box in the stable, and gave him some hay. Silver ate it daintily, and whinnied in a high shrill note which made George stare. The horses in the field came running to the gate to see the stranger, whinnying in reply, but when they heard his voice again, they galloped away as if in a fright.

The next day George took him to the meadows. Silver ran up and down the fields, swift as the wind. There never was such a racer. His long white tail streamed behind him like a flag, his delicate feet scarcely touched the ground. The heavy horses stood looking after him in astonishment, but they didn't offer to approach. In fact, they seemed alarmed and pressed against the comforting homely wood of the gate as they watched his capers.

"He's too silvery for them," explained George, as he stroked their sides and comforted them. "They don't like his colour." But that wasn't the reason.

The foal grew at a surprising rate under the care of George Greensleeve. His coat was like white satin with George's grooming, his legs were strong and straight, his movements were full of grandeur. Mrs. Greensleeve tried to spoil him with gifts of carrot and cake whenever she saw him, and he came up to the house and poked his nose through the window, asking for more.

George began to break him in as soon as he was old enough, and he led the prancing whinnying colt round the field at the end of a piece of rope. Silver went so fast that George was dragged like a scrap of paper, until his sister Ruth ran out and called to the colt. Then he stopped, and from that moment he was docile. He was quickly trained to the bridle, the saddle and words of command.

One day George noticed a change. A sharp point pierced the skin of Silver's forehead, and a white horn grew out like a tiny dagger. This horn became longer and longer, but it was beautiful, too. A slender spire of twisted ivory sprang from the centre of the horse's forehead, a dangerously long straight horn. At the same time Silver's coat became more like shining silver, so that at night, when he stood in the dark stable, or when he waited in the shadowy fields, he looked like a luminous horse from heaven's fields come down to earth.

Old Mr. Greensleeve wanted to cut off this horn, but George refused, for it was such a remarkable thing, and very useful in time of danger. He thought

9

he would like to go to the wars on Silver. Mrs. Greensleeve was afraid to give him sugar any more, lest he should poke the horn through the casement window, but little Ruth hung a daisy-chain round the horn. The horse tossed his head and stamped and pranced as if he realized how beautiful he was.

"You can't drive him to the village, George," exclaimed Mr. Greensleeve. "Not with that horn. Folks will laugh at you, and at him too."

"Let them laugh," cried George, boldly, but secretly he was shy of the remarks people might make. He waited some time, and then made up his mind to venture. He harnessed the silvery horse to the light trap and drove down the lanes to the village a few miles away. When they reached the high-road, the little horse ran so swiftly he left every cart and gig behind. People stared as the flashing steed sped by, but they only got a glimpse of the shining horn. When they approached the houses, George touched the rein. "Steady, Silver, steady," he cried, and the horse slackened his pace, dancing more slowly on his delicately-lifted feet.

The villagers shouted after, as George had feared they would. "Hi! George! What's that you're driving? Is it a horse? Are you come from a circus?"

The village policeman held up his big hand and stepped into the roadway.

"Hi! Stop! George Greensleeve! That's not allowed! What have you done to your horse?"

George pulled up the prancing Silver, which snorted and pawed the ground and waved his horn so fiercely that the policeman backed to a safe distance.

"This is Silver, my horse. Just an ordinary horse, but he's grown a horn! Any objection to that?" said George fiercely, and he gripped the reins and stared down at the fat startled policeman.

"That's no horse, don't tell me!" The policeman had been to a school where they taught natural history. "That's no horse," he repeated.

"Well, what is it, then?" asked George aggressively, for he loved Silver, and he determined to fight anyone who mocked at him.

"It's a unicorn! Or perhaps I ought to say, *an* unicorn!" said the solemn policeman.

"Well, what if he is? Amn't I allowed to drive a unicorn if I want? There's no law against it, is there?" asked George, who was pleased that Silver was such a romantic animal.

"No." The policeman scratched his head and consulted his notebook. "There ain't no law against unicorns, but you'll have to keep it off the shop windows and away from other horses. Look out!" A cart-horse went past with sidelong looks, his eyes rolling, his ears back, but the unicorn gazed ahead in a haughty manner.

George promised to look after his unicorn, and drove away to the barber's shop. He hitched the reins to a ring in the wall, and went inside for a haircut. A group of people gathered round. Doors opened, and mothers came hurrying from cottages. Children running home from school stopped to stare and point and laugh.

"How would you like to shoe that horse?" the baker asked the blacksmith.

The blacksmith with his leather apron round his

waist came from the forge and joined the group. "He's never been shod, and never will be," said he, looking with a professional eye at the unicorn's dainty feet. "I should have to make shoes of solid silver for that steed."

Some stroked the unicorn's flowing white mane, others admired his long tail, which George had left in all its silken beauty. Some bold ones tried to touch the horn, but the unicorn's eye flashed and the horn looked so dangerous, they retreated. Yet when little Annie Rose, the daughter of the farm bailiff, stretched up her hand, the unicorn put his head against her pinafore, and let her run her fingers up and down the twisty spiral as long as she wished, for a child could touch him when older people irritated him.

George came out with his hair trim and sleek, and there stood little Annie in the centre of the crowd, her arm around the unicorn's neck, her cheek against his side.

"She's like our Ruth," explained George. "She can do anything she likes with Silver. A little maiden can tame a unicorn."

In the field at the farm one day George noticed another peculiarity of the beast. The animal was more fastidious than the horses over his food and drink, and liked his water fresh from the spring, refusing all other. There was a muddy pool through which the cart-horses had splashed their great hooves. Silver dipped his horn in the turgid water, when immediately the pool became clear as crystal.

"Yes," said the policeman, when George boasted of this. "I've heard that unicorns have magical power in their horns." He knew all about their habits, and told George they came from India or Arabia, he wasn't sure which, but they were not much use on a farm, being too swift of foot and too particular.

One day a Fair and Wild Beast Show came to the village. The music of the merry-go-round, the whistle of the engine, the cries of the showmen with the coconuts and Aunt Sallies, rang through the air. Both George and Ruth wanted to go, so they dressed in their Sunday clothes.

"You'd better drive down with the old mare," cautioned Mr. Greensleeve. "It wouldn't be safe to take Silver into the crowd. You never know what might happen, and, with that long horn, there might be damage."

"I want folk to see my unicorn," protested George. "He's as good as gold when Ruth is with him. Folk don't have the chance to see a unicorn every day." So his father agreed, with some misgivings and headshakings.

It was a particularly fine Wild Beast Show which had honoured the little village with a visit. It would not have come, but this small place was midway between two market towns which were too far apart for a day's journey. Everyone for miles around went to see the show, and booths and stalls were set up in the market-place to add to the fun.

In the afternoon there was a grand procession, to attract the people to the night's performance. The show paraded down the village street, round the market-place, and past the duck pond and the village green. All the world stood watching, rich and poor, the squire, the blacksmith, the schoolmaster, policeman, tinsmith, cobbler, the saddler and the druggist, with their children, grandchildren, wives and aunts.

A mighty elephant marched first, with ponderous feet chained together, and a scarlet howdah on his back. A man who might have been a Hindoo, the onlookers were not sure, sat above the flapping ears. That was excitement enough without anything else, for none of the children had seen such a vast animal before. Next came a shaggy bear, a dancing bear with a muzzle over his nose, and a staff in his paws. Sometimes he shambled on all fours, sometimes he danced whilst his master beat a little red drum. The children clung to their mothers, and peered round corners of aprons and baskets; but next came a piebald pony with a golden-skirted lady sitting disdainfully on his back. Many a heart beat more quickly as she passed by. How beautiful she was! How dainty was her dress, spread out over the pony's back!

After her came the clown, a funny fellow with a chalk-white face and a red nose, and a tuft of hair on his head which bobbed gracefully to right and left. The children who had wept when they saw the bear, now began to laugh and point their fingers at him, for what do you think he did? He rode a donkey, and sat with his face towards the tail! Really, he was a funny man!

There were more ponies, little Shetlands, and dapplegreys, and bays, with monkeys and dogs on their backs. Finally came the chief attraction of the show, a forest-bred lion! He had never seen a forest, for he was born in the show, but that made no difference. He sat on a red-draped throne, drawn by four richly harnessed horses, and on his head he

14

wore a gold crown to show he was the king of beasts.

Cheers came from the crowd as the lion passed, and babies were held up in their mothers' arms to see the king of animals.

Now George and Ruth stood on the outskirts of the crowd, and George held the unicorn by the bridle. They were so much interested in the procession they forgot about their own Silver. George's eyes were wide as he stared at the elephant, the nimble monkeys, the bear and horses. He was enchanted by the golden girl and the comic clown, and the rein slipped from his grasp. Ruth, too, pressed nearer the front to see what was coming next.

The lion rode by, his eyes fixed ahead as if he saw those African forests of which his placard boasted. Suddenly there was a scattering of the crowd. The unicorn, with his shrill unearthly neigh, broke from George, snapped the traces, and rushed at the lion. The people screamed, the horses leapt to a gallop, the lion, rudely awakened from his day-dream, rolled from his throne, and the crown fell to the ground.

The unicorn impaled the symbol on his horn, but the lion resisted this indignity. Such a fight began as has never been seen before or since. The lion roared, but the unicorn, after the first challenging cry, was silent. With his pointed horn he stabbed at the lion, which crouched and sprang, only to miss the agile unicorn. Round and round the square they went, up the street and down, round the duck pond, and across the village green, in at the lych-gate, and out at the parson's wicket-gate. First the lion was the conqueror, and then the unicorn, and all the time the crowd tumbled about between them.

The people fled for safety to the shops and cottages, swarming up trees, clinging to the village cross. The booths and stalls were overturned, so that apples and gingerbreads, pears and sweetmeats rolled in the dust.

Tents were torn in tatters, and coconuts rolled about like so many brown heads. The empty merry-go-round turned noisily by itself. Aunt Sallies were scattered, and the big ninepins fell in the dust. The golden lady lost her wreath of flowers and clung weeping to the clown. The elephant ran trumpeting along the road, far away, to the terror of horses and cows in the fields.

At last the lion beat the unicorn, and forced him to the ground. He took back his crown, and placed it on his own head again, and then he gave a mighty roar of victory.

Some little boys ran up with white bread, and little girls with brown, and offered the loaves to the panting beasts. So much fighting had made them hungry, and it was better for the lion to eat bread than to devour children. Ruth found a plum-cake fallen off a stall, and she divided it between the two tired animals. She was just going to lead Silver back when the angry villagers drove both lion and unicorn away, out of the market-place, away from the merry-go-round, and the tumbled stalls, to a daisy field. The Wild West showmen slipped a chain round their lion and took him back to the show, with the crown safely on his head. George and Ruth captured their Silver, and harnessed him to the trap. There was no more Fair for them, and they drove home to tell their parents.

"I telled you so!" said Mr. Greensleeve. "You wouldn't be ruled by me, but I warned you! It will take fifty pounds to pay for all the damage that unicorn's done. Whatever did he attack a forest-bred lion for, and he so gentle, wouldn't hurt a lamb?"

"Because the lion said *he* was the king of beasts," replied Ruth indignantly; "and our unicorn is really the king. It was a *grand* fight! I looked through the window of Mrs. Wildgoose's shop, and didn't our Silver make that lion run! Didn't he put down his horn and beat off the lion! If it hadn't been for that ribbon stall which the unicorn upset, so that yards and yards of ribbon tangled him up and got round his horn, I think our Silver would have won, and we should have had the crown to keep. I would have hung it in the stable, over Silver's stall."

George said nothing, but groomed his pet, brushing off the mud, combing his knotted tail. Then he gave him fresh spring water and some oats. Mrs. Greensleeve came out with sugar and a carrot. The unicorn looked tired, but soon he was as speckless as ever, with his flowing mane, and his beautiful twisty horn.

Now the story of the fight spread throughout the length and breadth of England, and finally it reached the King's palace in London. His Majesty had always wanted a unicorn to run in his Park, so he sent a messenger to the farm.

"How much do you want for your unicorn?" asked the fine gentleman as he sat in the parlour and drank a mug of home-brewed ale.

"I don't want to sell him," answered George, decidedly.

"His Majesty the King wants to buy him for the Royal Park," said the messenger, and George stared to hear this. "He will give you a thousand pounds for the animal," continued he.

"That would just set up my mother and father," thought George, "and yet I love my unicorn, and I shall never have another."

"His Majesty will put a brass notice on the gate of the Park where the unicorn will live, and this is what it will say." He read from a sealed parchment which he carried, and Mr. and Mrs. Greensleeve and George and Ruth all stood up whilst he read the royal words.

"This unicorn, the last of its species, was trained by His Majesty's subject, George Greensleeve, of Windy Wood Farm, in the County of Derbyshire. It fought a lion and was defeated only after a great combat. It is worthy to bear the crown, along with the lion."

So George sold his unicorn to the King, and the messenger brought bags of gold for Mr. and Mrs. Greensleeve, so that they had no fear of want in their old age. The unicorn lived in London, in the King's Park, and all the little boys and girls went to look at him as he roamed among the trees and drank from the stream. They never tired of watching him dip his pointed horn and cleanse the water before he drank, so that a clear crystal brook ran through the grass.

Once a year George and Ruth came to see their Silver, and Ruth brought a daisy-chain to hang on his horn, and George a peck of oats grown on the farm. The unicorn rubbed his soft nose against their cheeks and pawed the ground with his little foot, as

if to say he had not forgotten the days of his youth,
when he frisked down the hilly fields and startled the
staid horses and the old mare.

On the Park gate was the brass notice, which
everyone read, and above it the King's arms, a lion
and a unicorn fighting for the crown, with the great
shield of England between them.

The little boys and girls of London read it aloud to their nurses, and then they sang this song:

> "*The Lion and the Unicorn,*
> *Fighting for the Crown,*
> *The Lion beat the Unicorn,*
> *And made him lie down.*
> *Some gave them white bread,*
> *Some gave them brown,*
> *Some gave them plum-cake,*
> *And drove them from the town.*"

The Crooked Man

In the village of Crick there lived, once upon a time, a homeless boy. Nobody knew where he came from, for one day, after a tribe of gypsies had passed with their dogs and horses, their caravans and carts, a poor little child was found wrapped in a piece of sacking, underneath a gorse-bush. He was brought up in the workhouse, and a more bedraggled twisted lttle fellow was never seen. He had bandy legs, crooked arms and a humped back. He was christened Thomas Furze, since it was under the furze-blossoms he was found, but the children called him the "Crooked Lad" or "Crooked Tim". Like a broken twig, or a wizened leaf he drifted quietly along the roads, under the hedgerows, up the lanes, seeking what he could find.

When he left the dame's school he had to earn his living, but all he could do was to scare the crows from Farmer Dale's ploughland. So there he sat on the stone walls, or he walked up and down the grassy verges of the fields, swinging his clacker and singing at the top of his shrill voice:

"O! All you little blacky-tops,
Pray don't you eat the farmer's crops.
Shua-O! Shua-O!"

All the crows flew away when they saw him, they were so frightened, for he was more like a living scarecrow than anything else, with his rags flapping and his thin arms waving.

He earned a penny a day for this work, and half a pint of milk, with some broken scraps of food. Now and then he caught a rabbit, or the farmer's wife gave him hot broth and a couple of eggs.

He took all home to the hovel where he lodged, and cooked his supper over his scanty fire. Somehow he managed to live, for his wants were few. He wandered over the meadows, looking for mushrooms and blackberries, for crabapples and sloes. He found flowers and fruit when other people passed by with unseeing eyes, for his sight was keen as a hawk's. His bright black eye spied the bird on the nest, the tiny field creatures running in the grass, the wild bee flying from its hole. He knew the names of herbs, too, pennycress, bedstraw, and shepherd's-purse, and he could make simples and cures from them, but where he got his knowledge no-one knew. Perhaps it was from his roaming ancestors, the gypsies, or he might have watched Old Biddy, the herb-doctor, for whom he sometimes worked. He made balsams and ointments for hurts and wounds, earning a few pence, but he was always poor and lonely.

One day he went up the fields, his sharp eyes as usual darting here and there, at hedge and ditch and wall. His hands were full of honeysuckle, his pockets brimmed with blackberries and nuts. As he walked his crooked way along the uneven grassy lane, he came to a stile. He wriggled between the tall narrow stones, and on the ground he saw something sparkle. He stooped down and picked up a sixpence, crooked as his own legs. There was a hole through it, where it had hung on somebody's watch-chain.

"A lucky bit!" cried the crooked little man, and he put it between his teeth to see if it was good, and rubbed it on his sleeve to polish it, and peered through the hole at the sun.

"This is the first time I've ever had a real piece of luck! What shall I buy with it?"

He pondered as he went along, and thought of all the things he liked. Dumplings, chitterlings, savoury-puddings, bull's-eyes, all made his mouth water. Or should he buy a tin whistle? The food would go, but the whistle would remain to cheer him when he sat rattling to the crows.

He carried the sixpence a week or two before he decided, and then he bought none of these things. In a cottage in the village lived a little sandy cat, a crooked humpbacked cat, which rubbed itself against his legs in such a friendly manner that he stopped and considered it. He stared at it for a minute or two, and a thought came into his poor tousled head. He stroked the little cat, and the animal purred and pressed close to him, and followed him. He went through the wicket-gate which shut out the garden with its clipped hedge, its neat flower-beds, and the shadowy light of the trees. He touched his cap, and said:

"Will you sell me your kitling, master? I'll give a sixpenny bit for her, if you'll part with her."

The man at the door looked at him and at the cat twining herself round his ankles.

"Why, it's Crooked Tom!" he cried. "You want that poor morsel? You can have her for nowt, and good riddance. We only keep her out of pity."

24

"Nay, I want to pay for her, and then she will be mine." Tom proudly held out his coin, shining and bright with all the polish he had given it.

"Have it your own way," laughed the man, and Tom went off with the crooked little cat running behind him, purring with all its might. The very first night it caught a mouse in the hovel, so Tom hadn't to provide it with any supper, which was just as well. Then it slept in his arms, and he curled up with the cat's warm fur against his cheek. He was glad he had bought the kitling instead of dumplings or whistles, he thought, as he felt the small heart throbbing, and the creature quivering with happiness and friendliness.

Months went by, and the crooked little man followed by his crooked little cat was a familiar sight. They explored fresh fields together, and wandered miles along the roads and overgrown lanes, always bringing back something new. Sometimes Tom took a basket of red crabs, or a capful of mushrooms to Mrs. Dale, the farmer's wife. Sometimes he twisted a hazel switch into a bow, and made arrows hardened in the fire and shafted with goose feathers for the farmer's little boy, or wove little green baskets of rushes for the young girl. He did all these things without thought of reward, just for the pleasure of speaking to human beings, or to get a glimpse of the kitchen fire, and a smell of the roast in the oven. All the time the crooked little cat grew, for the sunshine and exercise made her strong, and there was plenty of wild food for her. She became a splendid animal, fierce and strong as a small yellow tiger, with great eyes and thick golden fur.

25

Now the barns and cartsheds and stables were overrun with rats, and Farmer Dale was troubled about his grain and corn which disappeared as if an army were carrying it away. Holes appeared in bins and sacks, and trickles of oats and wheat lay on the floor.

"I'm fair mithered about the rats," said he, mournfully. "I've tried poison, and ferrets, cats, dogs and guns, but nothing keeps them down."

"The crooked man has a fine cat," said Mrs. Dale. "I should think it is a good ratter."

"I'll ask him about it," replied the farmer, and he went out to the fields, where Tom sat on a stone roller, waving his wooden clacker.

"She's a grand ratter," cried Tom, when he heard the farmer's request, "and I'd lend her to you with pleasure, but she won't stay anywhere without me." The great humped cat rubbed herself against his legs, and stared with her odd green and gold eyes at Mr. Dale. "I'll sleep in the barn," Tom continued. "It's a deal warmer than my own place, and the straw's a better bed, and cleaner, too."

So into the barn he went, and slept soundly, heedless of the scuttering and scampering and rioting which went on around him, but the next morning a pile of dead rats and mice told of the crooked cat's work. From barn to stable he went, and slept by the manger, from stable to cowhouse, from cowhouse to cartshed, and always the rats were cleared by the clever crooked cat.

"It's a grand life," exclaimed Tom, "to sleep with warm animals around you, and a good roof overhead, and a bowl of bread and milk for supper!"

The time came for him to return to his hovel, and he put his belongings into a small bundle and started off home. The farm was cleared of its vermin, and he had some shillings in his pocket.

Mrs. Dale watched him go, and then she turned to her husband. "The crooked man is a good-hearted creature," said she, "kind to the children, good to the beasts, and knowledgeable with herbs. His cat has done us a good turn."

"It's a champion cat, although it's crooked," replied the farmer, "and he's a likeable fellow, although his wits wander."

"He has no home," continued kindly Mrs. Dale, "nothing but that dirty hovel where he lodges. Couldn't he live in our empty cottage?"

"In that twisty old cot!" exclaimed her husband. "Well, nobody lives there, except hens and ducks. I could make room for them somewhere else. Yes, if you like, missis, he shall have the shepherd's old cot."

"Let it be a secret," cried the children, when they heard the news. "Let us make it all nice for him! Let us give him a big surprise!"

So they took buckets and brooms and whitewash, and soap and dusters and paintpots, and went to the tiny house, with its crooked oak timbers, its bent chimney, its deeply dipping thatch. The thatcher mended the roof with fresh yellow straw. Molly the milkmaid cleaned the house, and Mrs. Dale whitewashed the walls. The little boy put a coat of green paint on the dingy woodwork, and the little girl beeswaxed the twisted oak staircase. The windows were mended, the rafters were brushed, and in the

27

inglenook a great fire was lighted to air the kitchen. The floor was stoned with sand, the narrow garden path was weeded and swept, and a pile of firewood was left leaning against the side of the cottage.

Then Mrs. Dale looked in her attic at the farm, and brought out a crooked little rocking-chair, a twisty table, and a bed which was grand when its lost leg was replaced by a block of wood. The little girl collected old blankets, and the little boy took a frying-pan, a mug and a kettle. On the window-sill they set a scarlet geranium, and at the windows they hung blue curtains, faded to the colour of pale forget-me-nots, which they had found in their grandmother's ancient leather trunk.

Then they called the crooked man, who was starting off home after his work was done. He came round to the back door of the farm, his cap in his hand, his back bent, and his legs wobbling, whilst behind him stood the crooked sandy cat. He waited in the yard by the sycamore-tree, tired as he thought of the long trudge to his hovel, and the miserable room awaiting him there.

Out came Mrs. Dale and her children, carrying baskets covered with white cloths.

"We have something to show you, Tom. We hope you are not too tired to come with us across the pastures."

"No, ma'am, I'll come with pleasure," replied the little man. They went across the fields to the old cottage, with the crooked black timbers, and the odd bent chimney, from which came a curl of blue smoke.

"Who's living in the Crooked House?" wondered

the little man, but he was too polite to ask. They went up the narrow flagged path, and flung open the door. A bright fire burned on the open hearth, and the three-legged table was set for tea, with a queer little blue teapot and the blue mug. There was a lop-sided loaf of bread, a pat of butter, and a honeycomb. In the middle of the table was a bunch of wild flowers, and between the fluttering blue curtains glowed the pot of geraniums.

"This is your house now," said Mrs. Dale, laughing at the little man's cries of astonishment and delight. "You are to live here all your life. You can scare the crows, pick the herbs and flowers, cook your mushrooms, and do just as you like. You shall have new bread every baking-day, and as much curds and buttermilk as you want."

She uncovered the baskets and took out pots of jam and some brown eggs. Then she led him up the winding stair to see his little bed with the dimity cover, and the bent chair by the side. He looked with admiration at the snowy walls, and the clean scrubbed floor with its rag-rug and sheepskin mat. The cat walked about, wrinkling her nose, and purring in content. Suddenly she made a dash and caught a mouse which had dared to peep at the newcomers.

"Look! It's a crooked mouse," cried Mrs. Dale, and indeed it was! On its back was a tiny hump, and the cat carried the little creature carefully to her master without hurting it, and laid it at his feet.

"It shall live alongside us," said Crooked Tom, "and then we shall all be crooked together!"

From that day they lived all three in the crooked little house—the crooked man, the crooked cat, and the crooked little mouse, and there was nobody happier than they were, for they had no cares, but took whatever came with simple joy.

In time to come a song was made about them, and it was sung all over the countryside. Here it is:

There was a crooked man, and he walked a crooked mile,
He found a crooked sixpence upon a crooked stile,
He bought a crooked cat, and it caught a crooked mouse,
And they all lived together in a crooked little house.

The Four Brothers

Once upon a time, and that was very long ago, there lived a young girl named Sally. She had brown eyes and short dark hair, brushed like a boy's, and she was a chatterbox and a teaser. She lived at an inn, the "Hope and Anchor," an old timbered inn by the side of the great highway which goes to London one way, and to Scotland the other. It wasn't an ordinary inn, like the "Blue Bell," for Sally's father was an old sailor who had sailed round Cape Horn, and been to the China Seas. He wore gold ear-rings in his brown ears, and his beard was golden, too, pointed in a triangle, like Drake's.

In the garden he had a tall mast with a flag atop, and he hauled it up and let it down with ropes, and used strange sailor talk, such as country folk don't understand. There was a wooden figurehead of a heathen god, Neptune, leaning against the rockery under the fir trees, and this made all the little children come and stare and run away as fast as they could, for they thought the wooden man would catch them.

The inside of the inn was as clean as a pin, everything scrubbed white as a bone, and polished till you could see your face in it. That was Sally's task and the young servant girl's, for these two did nearly all the work between them. On the dresser was a model of a cutter, and on the mantelpiece were curious foreign shells, which roared like the waves of the

sea when you held them to your ears. Hanging over the window was a sailing-ship in a quart bottle, and this brought many a penny to the old sailor's pocket, as he showed it to his customers and told them yarns of the sea.

Sally was very proud of being a sailor's daughter, and the village children thought of her as a princess. They made her leader in their games, and she was chosen to be the May Queen when the first of May came round, all because her father was a sailorman in that village where hardly anyone had even seen the sea.

There were four lads, too, who were going to be sailors when they were old enough. Full of pranks they were, stealing apples from the orchards, climbing the haystacks, hanging the village washing on the treetops. They played tricks on the customers, too, did Matthew, Mark, Luke and John, whose saintly names were misplaced for such young scamps.

One of them had a frog-mug. Do you know what that is? A brown earthenware mug with a little green frog at the bottom. Matthew filled it with ale and gave it to an unsuspecting customer, who drank till he saw the frog's eyes staring at him, and its shiny back appear. Then there was a shout and great laughter at the joke.

More than anything they delighted in riddles, and these pleased the countrymen, whose minds were stored with old quips and jests, for this happened in days when there were few books, and riddle-telling was the winter's pastime.

"I went to the wood and got it. I sat down to look for it. I brought it home because I couldn't find it. What's that?" asked Matthew.

"A thorn," said the sailor, when no one could guess.

"In what place did the cock crow, when all the world could hear it?" asked Mark.

"On Noah's Ark," said somebody.

"What does a seventy-four gun ship weigh, with all her men on board, just before she sails?" asked Luke.

This was given up, and John told them: "Her anchor." Then the mugs of ale went round, tankards were filled afresh, songs were sung, and the "Hope and Anchor" got a reputation for wit and understanding.

When the four brothers were old enough, they all went to sea, and the village returned to its quiet ways, missing their pranks and noise. Sally was left alone with her father, for her mother had died when she was born. She cooked pease-pudding, and baked the bread, and made cowslip wine and cherry-brandy. She spun the snowy sheep's-wool on her spinning-wheel, and dyed the wool blue, and knitted her brothers each a pair of stockings ready for their return from their voyage to foreign parts.

"What will they bring me when they come back?" she asked her father.

"Oh, I don't know. Something queer, I expect," he answered, staring into the red fire. "Perhaps a poll parrot, same as I brought your mother, or a lump of coral, or an idol, or some silk." Sally went about her work, singing and sighing a little, and thinking very often of her four brave brothers over the sea.

After two years a letter came for Sally. Letters were rare events in those days, and Sally and her father broke the red seals, and spread out the paper on the little oak table in the bar-parlour, with a group of friends to listen to the news.

"My dear Sister Sally," went the letter. "We have had a good voyage, and seen some whales. I am bringing you a present. It is a goose without any bone. Your affec. brother, Matthew."

"A goose without a bone!" exclaimed Sally. "What a present! What kind of a bird will that be? Can it walk?"

"It must be some strange foreigner, perhaps a Chinese goose," said the linen-draper, and he turned over the letter and stared at the broken seals with their emblem of the rising sun.

"Where shall I keep the goose without any bone?" asked Sally. "I hope it will be able to swim in the duck pond."

She went about her work thinking of the queer bird which was coming over the sea, and all the village chattered and wondered. A parrot or a cockatoo would have been a nice gift for Sally, but a goose without any bone! Really, it was too silly! Only the old sailor was silent, with a secret smile as he listened to the talk.

A few weeks later there came another letter for Sally, and this had a blue seal, stamped with a ship in full sail. The girl opened it quickly and held it to the parlour window where geraniums and hanging white bells grew.

"Dear Sister Sally," said the letter. "We have had a good voyage, and seen some dolphins. I am bringing you a present when I come home. It is a cherry without any stone. Your affec. brother, Mark."

"A cherry without any stone!" cried Sally. "That's an odd present! I love cherries, but all cherries have stones. It isn't much to bring me all that way, is it, Father?" The sailor agreed that it wasn't much of a present, but "Wait and see," he advised.

"It's some outlandish foreign fruit your brother has found, although I never heard tell of a stoneless cherry, and I'm a man of considerable knowledge," said the squire's gardener. Sally polished and scrubbed,

35

and thought of the soft rosy cherries her brother Mark was bringing to her in the great sailing ship.

Now there came a third letter, with a green seal, and a ship's anchor on it. "This'll be from Luke," said Sally as she ran and called her father, and took it to the light.

"My dear Sister Sally," she read. "We have sailed round the world and seen some yellow men. I am bringing you a fine present. It is a blanket without any thread! Your affec. brother, Luke."

Sally read it three times, and then she looked at her smiling father. "Oh dear!" she sighed. "How Luke teases! That won't be warm at all," and all the customers in the bar-parlour repeated: "No warmth in that, Miss Sally! A blanket without any thread. Did you ever hear the like? Fancy that!" and they banged their mugs on the polished tables and asked for more of the nut-brown ale.

"It must be some kind of blanket they use in hot countries," explained the schoolmaster. "A tropical blanket, to keep off the flies," and all week Sally dreamed of a cobweb blanket hanging on a palm tree.

Finally a fourth letter came, a large square letter, sealed with a black seal, and a flying seagull upon it.

"This is brother John's writing," said Sally, contentedly, as she opened the letter. "He is more sensible than the others. I wonder what he will bring for me."

She read the letter aloud to her father and the company, all seated in the sunshine by the open door. "My dear Sister Sally," it said. "We are coming home soon after you get this. We have had a grand voyage and seen a sea-serpent. I am bringing you a beautiful present. It is a book no man can read. Your affec. brother, John."

Sally stamped her foot. "What is the use of that?" she cried. "A book no man can read. Why can't my brothers be serious?"

"Perhaps it's written in some foreign tongue, Greek, or double-Dutch," said the cobbler, and they all shook their heads over the strange odd languages in the world, which men spoke when they might talk honest English.

"Poor Miss Sally," said the blacksmith. "They've got you this time, fairly. What are your brothers bringing you? Tell us again."

So Sally repeated:

> "*A goose without any bone,*
> *A cherry without any stone.*
> *A blanket without any thread,*
> *A book no man can read.*"

They listened open-mouthed, and recalled the pranks and tricks the brothers had played when they were at home.

"Depend upon it, there is some joke in this, some mystification," said the old cobbler, who knew more than the schoolmaster and the parson. The sailor nodded his head and smiled. "Maybe," he agreed.

One fine day, up the hill which led to the inn came four sailor lads, with their trousers a-swinging, and their jaunty caps aslant on their heads, and their bundles slung on their backs. Sally ran out to meet them and flung her arms round each, kissing and clipping them all soundly. After her came the old sailor himself, full of laughter and joy to see his four sons again.

"You teasers!" cried Sally, when they had put their bundles on the floor, and stretched their legs by the house fire. "Where are those strange presents? We've all puzzled our heads off with wondering what they were. Where are the cherry, and bird, the blanket and book?"

"Coming up in the tranter's cart," replied John, winking at the others. "A blanket without any thread is heavy, you know." They all grinned, and Sally hugged him, happy to have him at home again.

Soon the bar-parlour of the "Hope and Anchor" was filled with men who had come in to drink the healths of the returned brothers, and Sally and the maid were kept busy running to and fro with the pewter tankards and earthenware mugs. There was a rumble of wheels at the door, and the tranter's cart came up.

"Now sit you still, Sally my dear, and we'll bring our presents in to you," said John, pushing her into the arm-chair, and the four boys went outside.

"Now we shall see," said the cobbler. "Now our eyes will be opened." He drank his ale and stood up ready to clap.

Matthew came in, carrying something hidden in his hands.

"The first is a goose without any bone," said Sally, as he stepped across the room to her.

"When the goose is in the eggshell there is no bone," said Matthew, and he held out a fine goose-egg to his amazed sister.

38

Next came Mark, with his mocking smile and twinkling blue eyes. "What was my present, Sally?" he asked, as he stood in the doorway, his hands hidden.

"The second is a cherry without any stone," replied Sally.

"When the cherry's in blossom there is no stone," said Mark, and he held out a small cherry-tree covered with snowy-petalled flowers, growing in a beautiful Eastern pot. Sally gave a cry of joy, and put it on the window-sill.

Then Luke put his head in at the door and muffled sounds came from outside, as if something struggled to get free.

"What was my present, Sally?" he asked, and his merry black eyes gleamed with amusement.

"The third is a blanket without any thread," said Sally.

Luke walked into the room leading a great white ram with amber eyes and a thick curly fleece on its back.

"When the fleece is on the sheep's back there is no thread," said the boy, and the ram jingled the bell at its neck and shook its horned head at the company of men who laughed and shouted and clapped their hands.

Finally John came in, young John with his brown hair, and bright kind eyes. "What was mine, Sally love?" he asked.

"The fourth is a book no man can read," said Sally, who looked like the Queen of Sheba with her gifts around her.

Then John bore in a little printing-press, with all

the letters backward. "When the book is in the press no man can read," said he, and everyone crowded round to look at the treasure, and to guess what was the tale in the press which no man could read.

Now the foreign goose-egg was set under the broody hen and in due time a wonderful gosling hatched out. It grew into the finest goose imaginable, with scarlet legs and snow-white wings, and a crest of red feathers on its head. It laid an egg every day, which the old sailor had fried for his breakfast. Yes— it was indeed a fine goose!

The cherry-tree was planted in the garden, and every spring it had masses of delicate blossoms, and every summer it was covered with rich fruit, different from country cherries, as full of sweetness as a hive is full of honey. Although there was never a stone in the flower, each cherry had a round hard heart.

The ram provided many a blanket from its heavy wool and it lived in the little square field at the back of the inn for many years. The inn has long since been pulled down, but the name of the field remains to remind us of this famous ram, for it is called "Blanket Croft" to this day.

As for the press, the story when printed was a strange tale of the Arabian Nights. Sally used it later to print her own little tales. One of the first she wrote was this, and the brothers sang it with her on Saturday nights to the visitors who came to see the wonders:

"*I had four brothers over the sea,*
  And they each brought a present unto me.
  The first brought a goose without any bone,
  The second a cherry without any stone,

The third a blanket without any thread,
The fourth a book no man can read.
When the cherry's in blossom there is no stone,
When the goose is in the egg there is no bone,
When the wool's on the ram's back there is no thread,
When the book's in the press, no man can read.

But the old sailor smiled to himself more than ever. "I just know'd 'em all along," said he. "I guessed 'em, every one of 'em," and he filled the frog-mug with his home-brewed ale and drank it up.

The Little Hen

Timothy Topp lived all alone in the cottage at the end of the wood. It wasn't really inside the wood, for there was a small field between the crowded trees and the cottage garden, but it was so close that Timothy could lean from his bedroom window and watch the cruel fox lurk under the wall, the rabbits play in the sunlit glade, and the wood-pigeons preen their wings in the beech-trees.

It was the prettiest cottage you ever saw, and very convenient, for it had two rooms upstairs and two down, and the cosy kitchen opened straight into the garden, which had borders right and left of the paved path, and rose-trees and currant-bushes, cabbages and sweet-williams.

At the back of the cottage was another field, which belonged to Timothy, and in it were three old apple-trees which carried a clothes-line, and a small hay-stack fenced round. Timothy thought it was a para-dise for two—for himself and Betty Bond, whom he dearly loved.

"Will you marry me, Betty?" he asked every Wednesday night, when she was free to walk out with her young man, and they strolled through the woods to gather primroses and violets.

"Yes, I will, Timothy," answered Betty, giving him a kiss, and they walked contentedly among the rustling leaves, with blackbirds and tomtits overhead,

43

and they made plans about the cottage they had seen to let. That was where they intended to live some day.

"Will you marry me, Betty?" asked Timothy Topp on Saturday night, when Betty had her second free evening, and they walked through the bright streets of the market town where Betty was in service.

"No, I won't, Timothy," answered Betty, giving him a poke with her elbow, and they went into the playhouse and watched the pretty ladies and fine gentlemen on the stage with the red velvet curtains. They sucked humbugs and lollipops, and sat close together on the hard bench at the back of the room, but Timothy sighed because he could not afford these delights for Betty, and she sighed because she couldn't bear to leave them behind and go to live in the country.

Yet, when Wednesday came, and they wandered through the green loveliness, she changed her mind and said "Yes", but on Saturday her answer was "No". Timothy went pale with the constant changing of Betty. She was like the moon, never the same for two weeks running.

At last Timothy went to live in the cottage alone, hoping that Betty would make up her mind to get married very soon. Alas! She *did* make up that wavering mind of hers, but not in the way Timothy hoped, for she decided to marry the policeman, if he would ask her.

He walked up and down her street every day, and guarded her from robbers and highwaymen. He saw her bright eyes peeping at him from under her white cap, and he heard her pretty voice. With him she went to the playhouse once a week to see romances of high life, and Timothy was left alone. Not quite alone, however, for he had sixty hens, a couple of golden cocks, a fine sow and thirteen little pigs. He couldn't be really lonely with so many noisy little friends.

Timothy earned his living by keeping a stall at the market. On Tuesdays and Saturdays he went there with his basket of eggs, a few rabbits, and some bunches of flowers, roses and lilies, sweet peas and pinks, with green and white ribbon-grass waving among them. Everyone wanted a bunch of country flowers from Timothy's stall. He took cherries and currants, blackberries and mushrooms, too, according to the season, and made quite a nice bit of money which he put in a stocking and hid in the parlour chimney.

Sometimes he saw Betty in the distance, but she took no notice of him, for she was soon to be the policeman's bride, to live in a little red-brick house with a brass door-knob, and "County Constabulary" outside to tell everyone who she was. She had forgotten the smell of primroses and wet leaves, and the feeling of the scented wind on her cheeks.

"I can't abide the town," said Timothy to himself. "Not for more than a day. It's no good. I wouldn't live here, not if it was ever so," which meant "not if it were perfect". He marched home again along the roads and lanes and field-paths to his cottage by the wood.

Now Timothy could manage the outside work very well, and he kept the garden trim and the little yard tidy, but the inside of the house bothered him.

When he was out of doors, things went wrong. The fire died out, the cat licked the dishes, the bed remained unmade, dinner was forgotten, and dust collected on chairs and shelves, although the air was crystal clean. Timothy struggled, but "My fingers are all thumbs", he complained to Jack Stone, his neighbour down the valley.

"You ought to get wed, Timothy," replied Jack, but Timothy shook his head. "Nay. I shall manage without a woman now," and he struggled along, washing and ironing, and sweeping as well as he could.

One day, when he was returning home from market with his empty baskets on his arms, he thought wearily: "When I get in, I shall have to light the fire, and trim the lamp, and wash my dishes left from breakfast, and make my bed, and cook my tea, and wash up again, and darn my stockings, and stitch on a few buttons, and feed the hens and pigs, and set a rat-trap, and mend the fence, all before I go out shooting. It will be midnight before I can get to bed!"

He sighed deeply, and went on. "Tomorrow I must go to the mill and get some flour, and buy a sitting of duck-eggs, and——" but the list was so long he hadn't finished when he walked through the wicket-gate to his garden. There he cheered up. "It's a nice little house," said he, forgetting all his troubles as he walked up the garden path, stooping to lift a fallen flower, to taste a berry, to remove a weed.

The dog barked joyously, and he unloosed him from the kennel. The cat came mewing down the stairs of the outside loft. The hens ran from every corner of the field, cackling to be fed, and he put down his baskets and attended to his animals before he went indoors to the disorder he had left early that morning. Feeding, watering, talking to them, he felt quite happy again.

Then he unlocked the door and stepped inside.

What was this? The room was swept clean and there was never a speck of dust. The dirty breakfast things which he had left on the table were washed and put away. On the table lay a row of twenty little white loaves of bread, newly baked, and each loaf was in the shape of an egg. He picked one up, sniffed at the good smell, and ate it, with exclamations of wonder.

"Who's done this?" he cried, peering about. Then he thought of his money and ran to the parlour, but the stocking was safe up the chimney. No kindly burglar had been there to rob him after dusting his rooms. Upstairs the bed was made, the room was swept, his hair brush was put tidily away, his dirty collar hung clean and ironed on a chair-back, and his stockings were washed and mended!

He hurried downstairs again, and looked round for an explanation. "Is it a fairy? Is it one of those lob-lie-by-the-fires I heard about when I was a youngster?" he asked himself wonderingly. "It can't be Betty, for she is at work, and she's forgotten all about me."

Then a little movement startled him. In a corner of the hearth sat a red hen with bright eyes and shiny smooth feathers. He knew her at once, for she was one of his favourites. She always ran first to welcome him, and he had missed her when he fed

47

the flock. She was so clean, so jimp, so lissome, so quiet among the noisy blustering crowd, he always kept a special morsel for her.

"What are you doing here, Jinny?" he asked. She gave a low cluck and walked through the door.

"I expect she flew through the window looking for crumbs," said Timothy. "I'm glad that whoever's been here hasn't taken my little red hen." He boiled the kettle and sat down to tea. He ate the oval cobs, and toasted a piece of cheese, and then he went out to his work.

All evening he was mystified, but he found no trace of a footprint near the house. His work was quickly done, and as he tidied the garden he whistled happily.

The next day he went through the wood to the mill for flour and the sitting of duck-eggs. When he came back everything was tidy again, but the rocking-chair swayed backwards and forwards as he entered the kitchen. He slipped softly up to it, and there sat the little red hen, with her eyes shut, rocking to and fro in a dream. Even then he did not guess who had done the work, for often a stray hen got into the house, so he shooed her out, and shut the door. In the oven were the little loaves, baking all by themselves, and piled up were the clean dishes. It was amazing! He went about the house with watchful eyes, listening and looking for a dwarf with a broom-stick and a cocked hat, but, as before, there was nobody.

He had his dinner and worked in the garden, but all the time he kept one eye on the house. After a while he put down his fork and crept to the window.

48

What a strange sight! There was the little red hen, as you have guessed, with a tiny brush of heather, sweeping the floor, picking up the crumbs, and tidying all away. She flew with a small feathery mop to the sink and washed all the dishes. Then she flew with a towel and dried them. She carried the flour to the bowl, a scrap at a time, stirred in the warm yeast, and set the bread to rise. Then she shaped the dough into egg-like loaves, and put them in the oven.

"So it's my little red hen that's the good fairy, is it?" cried Timothy, and the hen clucked "Yes!"

From that time Timothy Topp was never really lonely, for he had the jolliest little companion in the world. She was never cross, or scolding, she never grumbled when he came in with dirty boots. Quietly she brushed and cleaned them, crouched on the brown sanded hearth at his feet. When he sank down tired, she made a cup of tea, with a tiny little kettle, no bigger than a pill-box. She brewed delicious ale from dandelions and nettles, and made ointments from little flowers she found in the fields. She sewed and baked and mended with tiny white stitches, and flew on errands for him, so that Timothy's life would have been all happiness, if his love for Betty had not kept him awake at nights.

One day he sat by his bright fire, with the grate shining, and his table well set. There was a clean cloth, and pink and white china, little cobs like new-laid eggs, and a couple of brown eggs besides. The cup and saucer gleamed in the firelight, the teapot shone like silver. In the middle of the table was a jug of mignonette and cornflowers, and on a chair near Timothy perched the little red hen, her feathers like burnished copper.

Suddenly footsteps came up the path. The dog barked, and there was a knock at the door. The hen flew under the table, and Timothy went with beating heart to see who it was, for he thought he knew that step! There stood Betty Bond!

"Can I come in, Timothy?" she asked, sadly.

"Do you still want me, Timothy?" said she, as she sat down in the chair the little red hen had just left.

"That I do, Betty dear." Timothy leaned over her and stroked her hair.

"Well, I'll marry you as soon as you like," said Betty. "I found my mistake. I don't love anyone but you, and I don't want the town any longer." She burst into tears.

"But the policeman?" asked Timothy, bewildered.

"He wants to marry a Columbine girl, who dances on one leg in the playhouse. He says I'm too coun- trified. My heart isn't his, and he is right. It's yours, Timothy, if you'll have it."

"Of course I'll have it, my Betty," cried the delighted young man. "I'll go to the parson and have the banns called, and then we'll get married."

"But how do you manage to keep all so tidy, so beautifully clean, Timothy?" asked Betty suspi- ciously, as she dried her tears on his sleeve.

"I'll show you," answered Timothy. He called "Cluck! Cluck! Cluck!" under the table, but there was no answer. The little red hen had gone. There she was, pecking in the field with the others, an ordinary little fowl again. Her work was done, and she didn't intend to interfere with a real housewife.

So Timothy married Betty, and they lived happily in the little house at the end of the wood all their lives. Mistress Betty kept the house neat and clean, and mended Timothy's clothes, and looked after the children like a good mother.

On Saturday nights Timothy used to take the children on his knee after their baths, and tell them about the little red hen which had once lived with him and taken care of him when he had no Betty.

He always ended the story with a song, which they sang together. This is it:

"I had a little hen, the prettiest ever seen,
 She washed me the dishes and kept the house clean.
 She went to the mill to fetch me some flour,
 She brought it home in less than an hour;
 She baked me my bread, she brewed me my ale,
 She sat by the fire, and told many a fine tale."

As for the little hen, she lived for many a year, and when at last she died, Timothy and Betty put a tombstone over her grave, and wrote the song upon it.

Wee Willie Winkie

"Wee Willie, you must go to sleep at once," exclaimed Mrs. Winkie, as she shook the feather-bed and straightened the pillows in the attic of the church tower.

"I can't sleep yet, mother. You know I can't. What would the children do if I forgot them? The naughty ones wouldn't go to bed at all! They depend on me to rap and call." Willie sat up in his truckle-bed, and ran his fingers through his curly mop. He hadn't to wait very long now, for the beams of the bright moon were moving across the wall.

Mrs. Winkie went to the slit, where many an arrow had flown in ancient days. She looked down from the height of the tower at the streets of little houses, with lighted windows and tightly-shut doors. Sounds of laughter and song, shouts of many children came through the night air. An owl brushed past and flew from the rafters above the bed. The church bells murmured in the wind which blew about the cobwebbed room.

"Now I'll put a shade over the moon, dear, just a little cloud, and you must go to sleep," said Mrs. Winkie, but Wee Willie scrambled to the floor and flung his arms round her neck.

"Mother! Let me go! It's eight o'clock," he cried. "The stars have all come out, and it's time for me to go."

"All right, then, but be quick and get back before the Great Bear treads on your tail. He's there, high in the sky."

"That's the worst of having a dream-child, he has so many duties," she sighed, as Wee Willie dashed to the door. He ran pitter-patter down the dark dusty bat-haunted stairs of the church tower, threw open the great oaken door, and fluttered like a white bird into the street. His white nightgown floated behind him, his yellow hair stuck out like a frill of gold. The moon stared down and winked at him, for she knew him very well indeed. The stars blinked their eyes and said: "There goes Wee Willie Winkie about his bedtime work."

The old watchman at the corner turned up his collar, and flashed his lamp on the boy, who ran past like a dancing autumn leaf.

"Eight of the clock and a fine starlit night," he called in a great voice which boomed through the streets and lanes like a bell, for in those days the watchmen told the hours and guarded the towns through the nights.

"Wee Willie Winkie's just on the dot tonight," said he to himself, and then he stumped up the street to look for robbers and footpads, and to talk to his cronies, the other watchmen.

All the very best children had been in bed an hour or more, but many were sitting in bath tubs, being scrubbed and rubbed. Some were eating their bread and milk, dipping wooden spoons into the steamy mixture, and popping them into round red mouths. Some were sitting on their mothers' and nurses' knees, listening to the story of "The Babes in the

Wood", or "Cinderella". Some were stamping angry little feet, struggling and crying: "I *won't* go to bed. I won't! I won't!" Some were hiding behind curtains or under chairs, hoping no one would notice them and send them to bed. But every child had one ear cocked, listening for Wee Willie Winkie's call.

Wee Willie began at Number One, and ran down the streets, calling at each house, putting his little mouth to the keyholes, and singing through the locks of the front doors, "Are the children in their beds? It's past eight o'clock."

In each house there was a race and scramble. Every child hastened to obey that sleepy slumber-voice, and tumbled into bed without waiting to finish supper, or even to get properly undressed. Socks were pulled off, shoes thrown in corners, nobody must be up after Wee Willie Winkie had called through the lock, or tapped with his small fist at the window-pane.

Up and down the streets ran the elf-like boy, and his nightgown flapped like feathers round his legs, his voice piped like the eerie wind.

"There's Wee Willie Winkie," warned the mothers, and they undressed the sleepy children, whose eyes were half-shut, and lifted them into bed. They blew out the candles, and shut the bedroom doors, sighing with relief, "What should we do without Wee Willie Winkie to bring sleep to our bairns?" In a few minutes there was silence. Every child was abed, the town was asleep. Little Willie Winkie ran fast with his bare feet scarcely touching the pavements. He darted through the church door, and up the winding stair. He snuggled down in the belfry, and fell asleep himself in one minute, for he was Sleep's own son.

In one cottage a little boy didn't go to bed. He was crouched in a hiding place, and nobody saw him. "Is Thomas abed?" asked his busy mother, as she stooped over her ironing. Nobody answered, so she went on with her work. All those frilled shirts and crisply starched petticoats and long white nightgowns to be ready for the next day. Two clothes-basketfuls lay under the table, and she thumped her iron up and down and glanced at the baby in the cradle by the fire. Under the table sat Thomas, quiet as a mouse, wedged between the baskets, waiting to escape. He had heard Willie Winkie's call to sleep, but he wanted to see what there was out of doors after the magical bedtime hour of eight o'clock. In his pocket he had stored a halfpenny loaf, for he knew he would be hungry on his adventures.

Somebody left the street door open, and Thomas's mother turned her back as she hung a nightshirt up to the fire and then bent over her baby. Thomas crept out on all fours, like a little dog, through the open doorway, and off!

He ran very fast down the hill for a few minutes till he had left his home safely behind. He reached the bridge, and the river lapped below him, flapping gently like a pair of old slippers, slapping against the stones, murmuring and whispering secrets. There were dipping willows down there, too, and big houses by the waterside. All was very quiet, and he crept into one of the corners of the bridge, an embrasure over a buttress. Deep in the water he could see stars, and up in the heavens were more stars, and although he tried to count them, there wasn't time. A great moon hung like an orange, and a gold path of moonlight lay on the water. In a willow an owl hooted, and a couple of flittermice darted over Thomas's head and squeaked in his hair. The night watchman passed by, and Thomas crouched still in the shadow, his heart thudding lest he should be found.

Under the wall at the bottom of a river-garden was a small ladder, shining like a silver thing in the moonlight. Thomas dragged it to the house and climbed up to look in at the window. Like a dusky cat he crept up and pressed his nose to the pane.

In the nursery lay two little girls fast asleep, with their hair in short plaits, and the sheets tucked up to their chins. Thomas tapped gently till they opened their eyes.

"Come out and play," he called, and they sat up in bed, staring at the little boy outside.

"Come out and play, the moon doth shine as bright as day," sang Thomas, in a fluting sweet voice, and they ran across the floor, and slipped through the window to him, and climbed down the ladder.

They carried it next door, and ran up like *three* little cats. Soon two more children joined them, and came sliding down, eager to wake up others, and to play under that golden moon. Round the town they went, carrying the little ladder, keeping to the gardens, hiding in the moon-shadows, a little band of nightgowned children, ever growing more and more till only the babies were left in bed.

Then they played "Catch", and "Hide-and-Seek".
Up the ladder and over the walls, across the bridge,
hiding in the little cornered houses upon it, then
back to the streets they went. They slid and danced,
they skipped and flew, for the strange thing was that
they found they had wings under their nightgowns,
mysteriously grown in the night by the power of
that round gold moon!

Little voices rang, little feet jigged, little heads
wagged. The night watchman came down the hill
and crossed the bridge again.

"Nine o'clock by the night, and a fine moonlit
night," he called, and the children mocked him, and
flouted him, and laughed at him with tinkling laughter, but he never heard a sound. Perhaps he was
deaf; perhaps the children were invisible as they
swung in the trees, and leapt in and out of the
shadows.

At ten o'clock they clustered like bees round their
leader, Thomas the washerwoman's son.

"We're hungry," they cried. "We want some
supper." Then Thomas took the halfpenny loaf from
his pocket, for he was, of course, the only one who
was dressed and *had* a pocket, and he broke it in
little pieces for them. They held up their portions
in the moonlight, and it was silver bread, and it
tasted like honeycomb. They drank from a fountain
in the market square, sipping in turn from the iron
cup which hung chained to the lion's head, where the
water gushed. The moonlight had turned it to silver
water, and they drank and drank again.

Then their revels grew wilder, and they ran in and
out round the town, leaping like ponies over gates

and walls, flying like birds over fences and hedges, floating like fishes in the calm moonlit air. They played "Follow-my-leader", with Thomas as leader, and "Orange and Lemon", and "I wrote a letter to my love".

Eleven o'clock was chanted in that bell-like voice, and they sat in a circle round the watchman's fire. He, poor man, tramped the distances, seeking the cause of all the restlessness in the air, the strange flickering white movements he had glimpsed, the rush past of unseen pattering bare feet, the unsettled barking of the town dogs. The little company sat close together, warm and snug, and Thomas told them the story of "The Three Bears". Then every little boy and girl told a tale, and some were so short they had only a few words in them, and some were so long they never ended. Then the watchman's voice was heard calling "Twelve of the clock, and a fine moonlit night," and his heavy tread approached.

The children all stood up, and taking hands, they sang together in chorus:

> " Boys and girls come out to play,
> The moon doth shine as bright as day.
> Leave your supper and leave your sleep,
> And join your playfellows down the street.
> Come with a whoop, and come with a call,
> Come with a goodwill or not at all.
> Up the ladder and down the wall,
> A halfpenny loaf will serve us all."

Now their voices were so clear and so shrill that although the watchman did not hear them, Wee

Willie Winkie up in the church tower turned in his
sleep. He shuffled and sat up. He sprang out of bed,
and ran down the windy stairs, his gold locks on
end, his arms waving with indignation. Out of doors
he rushed like a little hurricane, up and down the
town, till he found the gathering of children dancing
round the watchman's fire.

"Shoo! Shoo! Shoo!" he cried, flapping his arms,
and all the children flew like white pigeons, across
the market square, back through their windows into
their beds.

"What's this?" cried Thomas's mother, as she drew
out the last shirt from the basket at midnight. "What's
this?" There lay Thomas, curled up on the floor, his
head on his arm, his dirty little boots tucked under him.

"Poor bairn! He must be tired to sleep like this under the table. I never missed him!" said she, and she undressed her son by the dying fire and carried him up to bed with her.

The next day every child in the town was late for school. Nobody knew the reason for the tired legs and the sleepy eyes, but we know, don't we? It was because they disobeyed Wee Willie Winkie!

Wee Willie Winkie ran through the town,
Upstairs and downstairs in his nightgown,
Knocking at the windows, calling through the locks,
"Are the children in their beds? It's past eight
o'clock!"

The Cat and the Fiddle

Shutters were fastened, doors locked, the rug was rolled back from the hearth, the groaning weights were pulled up to the top of the grandfather clock, and the lamp was extinguished. The family picked up their candlesticks and walked up the wooden stairs to bed, leaving the kitchen to the silence of the night.

The fire flickered with little points of flame, the clock ticked solemnly as it listened to the sounds which came from upstairs, the thump of bare feet on the floor above, the scrape of a chair, and then a thud as somebody got into bed.

Tick! Tock! went the old clock, louder and louder, and his brass face shone in the falling light of the fire. There was a scurry of little feet across the floor as a couple of mice came dancing through a hole in the wainscot, and raced to the flour-bag which stood wide open on the pantry bench.

The cat roused herself and looked after them.

"Never mind," said she. "Not tonight. I've something better to do than to chase two skinny mice. Tomorrow they will be fatter. Besides, I had a good basin of bread and milk."

She sighed happily, and stretched her legs in the warmth of the hearthstone. Then she yawned, listened intently to the snores in the room above, and stood up. She crept under the old settle in the corner of the room, and walked about among the boots and shoes which lay scattered there. Sometimes a mouse moved in the toe of one of the farm boots, but she turned aside from temptation, and peered into the stick box. From a pile of kindling chips she lifted out a curiously-shaped piece of wood, and carried it back to the hearth. It wasn't a stick at all, it was a fiddle, a roughly shaped little fiddle with four strings of horsehair drawn tightly across the tiny wooden bridge.

She held it under her furry chin, and twanged with her claws, but the noise did not please her, so she went under the settle again and brought out a slim stick for a bow. She tuned the four strings, holding her fiddle to her ear, and then she began. She played a little odd air, a queer jumpy kind of tune, and the clock stared down and ticked louder than ever.

The lading-can shuffled its tin sides, as it lay on the sink, and slowly rocked like a boat at sea, clanging softly on the stone. The wooden milk-bowl beat its sides. The nutmeg-grater scraped and sawed with a nutmeg, the blow-bellows puffed, and the egg-beater began to whirr, as the music from the little fiddle welled through the kitchen and waked all the sleeping pots and pans.

On the hob the great copper-kettle sang a shrill high song, and the water began to boil. As the steam came out, the lid rattled up and down like a dancing ninny. Saucepan-lids jingled like tambourines as they hung in a row on the wall, and the walking-sticks in the corner rapped with little feet and tripped out into the middle of the floor.

The cat glanced round and nodded approvingly.

It was better than she expected. She changed her tune to a merry jig, a country dance of long ago. Down leapt the saucepan-lids, and down sprang the gleaming silvery dish-covers. They could hang there no longer, and they clattered round the blue and red tiled floor with the pewter salt-pot and pepper-box.

"Do keep still, pepper," sneezed the cat. "I can't play when you dance." So the pepper-box stood in a far corner near the big milk cans and beat time with his round little head.

The eyes of the clock were agoggle, and he held his hands in front of his face in amazement at the capers of some of the kitchen things. He had thought they were so quiet and modest, and here they were, jigging up and down like morris-dancers at the fair. He had seen nothing like it since he was born.

The flat-irons burst open the door of the ironing cupboard, and joined in the dance. Everyone kept away from their heavy feet, but the tiniest crimping-iron was a great favourite, she was so lively.

There was a movement on the high mantelpiece, and all the brass candlesticks leaned forward, peeping down at the commotion below. The kitchen floor was like a ballroom, and they longed to join the fun, There wasn't room to dance on the narrow ledge where they stood, but it was a long way down to the ground. Could they jump it? They stooped and held out their flat brazen skirts. The copper pestle-and-mortar in the middle of the mantelpiece counted for the jump. Three hundred years is a great age, and he was content to look on.

"One to be ready! Two to be steady! Three to be *off*!" he shouted, and down they all fell with a great clatter, and danced more gaily than anyone in their shining brass petticoats and their tall extinguisher hats. They knew all the old country dances, for they had watched them in bygone days, and they showed the younger members the stately measures of Queen Bess's reign.

The cat played "Lady Greensleeves", and "Here we go round the Mulberry Bush", and "Over the Hills and Far Away", and all the tunes you have ever heard. She was a musical cat. She had listened to the songs the children sang when they sat with their mother at the piano in the parlour. They didn't know she took any notice, for she lay on the broad window-sill, with her green eyes fixed on the birds in the garden. But her ears twitched, and the little songs went into them, and there they stayed, waiting in her memory till she could make music herself.

Now, all the time she played, there was a subdued squeaking and a muffled whispering on the oak dresser. It came from the long wooden box which lay near the open knife-box. The knives had gone long ago, and were hopping on the floor in glittering rows, but this finely polished oaken box had a heavy lid. Sometimes it moved up a little, and then it sank down again. Evidently something was trying to get out, for bright eyes peered through the crack, and then disappeared, and the struggle began again.

"All together! Heave! Heave-O!" cried a tiny tinkling voice, and the lid shot up. Out scrambled a company of spoons and forks, with a clitter-clatter, and soon they scampered across the dresser. They swarmed down the carved legs, and joined the assembly on the floor. They were the best dancers of all, and they twirled round with each other, with the nutmeg-grater, the egg-beater, and the toasting-fork. One big wooden spoon, used for stirring the jam in the enormous brass pan, actually danced with the frying-pan!

Pussy played a waltz, so sweet and dreamy that the willow-pattern dishes from the dresser shelf, and the blue cups and lustre-jugs hanging on the hooks, stepped lightly down with never a crack, and whirled round in rapture. Even the great iron key of the door waltzed round in the lock and then fell to the floor with a clang.

"Oh!" it cried. "Do let me join in this lovely whirligig"—for that was the name it gave the waltz, which was new in those days—and it whirled round with the key of the stable-door, which had jumped from the end of the dresser where the stable-boy had put it for the night.

When the door-key turned in the lock, the door came open, and little cold night-winds slipped into the kitchen, sending the dying flames roaring up the chimney afresh, blowing the little dancers here and there. The cat looked up, and walked to the door-way, playing her fiddle as she went.

"Shut the door! Shut the door!" cried the candle-sticks. "We don't like draughts!"

"Hush!" whispered the cat, softly. "Hush! Come and look out of doors, all of you. Come and look at the full moon."

So the crowd of little pots and pans, dishes and jugs, spoons and knives and forks, swayed to the doorway, and gazed up into the sky. There, high up in the blue starry night-sky, above the stables and cowsheds and weathercock, hung a great yellow moon, a moon of gold, looking down and actually smiling at them!

They all waved to the moon, and bowed three times over their left shoulder, for it was the first time some of them had ever seen her, and they wished to pay her homage in the ancient way.

"We see her very often from the attic windows," boasted the candlesticks, but they bowed just the same. The little crimping-iron was much impressed by her glory, and touched the ground with her nose, and the cat laid her paw on her heart, and bent down with her fiddle sweeping the earth. She knew the moon very well. She could almost call herself a personal friend of the moon's!

In the orchard stood Sally the cow, and at that moment she, too, raised her head and stared at the golden moon. Rover the house-dog came out of his kennel to see what was the matter.

"Hush!" whispered the cat again. "Look yonder!"

Sally the cow suddenly tossed her head, flicked her tail, and galloped across the orchard. Then she took a leap, and flew up in the air, higher than the apple-trees, higher than the weathercock on the barn end. Up she sailed, and all the pots and pans cried, "Oh-oo-oo-oh!" and opened wide their eyes.

Over the moon went Sally, and then she came spinning down to earth again, and dropped among the apple-trees where she started. She went on eating as if nothing had happened, but Rover the dog laughed and laughed as if he would never stop, and all the little dancers clapped their tiny hands.

The cat took up her fiddle and began to play,

68

when, through the open door, down the path to the wicket-gate, and across the cobbled yard, ran an odd couple.

"Now's our chance," whispered the willow-pattern dish. "Will you come with me, beautiful one? Will you run away in the moonshine? It's the one chance in our lives. Never again will the door be open and the way clear as it is tonight."

"I'll go to the world's end," sighed the loving spoon, and hand in hand they pattered over the grass to freedom. Down the steps by the orchard they ran, and across the field into the lane, and away.

The moon drew a cloud over her face. Rover crept into his kennel. The cow lay down on the dewy grass and composed herself to much needed sleep. The cat put her fiddle under her arm and returned to the kitchen. All the pots and pans and tins climbed sedately and silently back to their places. The candlesticks clambered up the wall and clasped the mantelpiece to swing themselves up onto it. The spoons, with many a struggle, managed to lift the lid of the spoon-box, and slipped inside whispering of their missing sister. The flat-irons opened the cupboard door and went inside to the darkness, with the little crimping-iron whose heart thumped with excitement.

"What a romance!" she cried; but "Hush! What a disgrace!" said the other irons.

"It all comes of dancing," exclaimed the pestle-and-mortar, when the candlesticks told him about it, but he wished he had seen the elopement, all the same. It reminded him of the time when the pretty young daughter of the house slipped away at mid-night with the squire's son, exactly two hundred years ago.

But the key returned to the lock, and the fire died down. Pussy fell asleep, and slept so soundly that the two little mice, who had been eating in the flour-bag during the great dance, now came out again, and boldly jigged round the tired animal!

As they jigged, they heard a little song, a tiny coppery song, which came from the mantelpiece. They looked up and saw the ancient pestle-and-mortar, with open mouth, chanting this lay:

> "*Hey diddle diddle!*
> *The cat and the fiddle.*
> *The cow jumped over the moon.*
> *The little dog laughed to see such fun,*
> *And the dish ran away with the spoon!*"

But alas! the dish and the spoon didn't go far. John, the farmer's son, found them at the bottom of the lane the next day. The poor dish was broken by the rough stones, and the spoon was bent. It was a sad ending to a honeymoon, but they had their romance.

Four and Twenty Tailors

M r. Stitch the tailor sat cross-legged in his little front room, sewing with needle and thread the breeches of Mr. Oats the farmer. In and out went the needle, and as he sewed he hummed a tune to himself, for he felt at peace with the world. He moved his spectacles up on his forehead, and glanced through the window which looked on the narrow street, where old overhanging houses leaned across the road as if they were talking to one another. Every now and then a cart went by, with a clip-clop-clop of horses' hooves, and a rumble-dumble of wheels on the cobblestones. Sometimes a friend passed, tapping at the glass, and calling "How do, Samuel?" and Mr. Stitch nodded in a dignified way, and answered "How do?"

"Wife, wife," he called at last, for evening was dropping her shadows, and there were no lamps in the street. "Wife. Bring a light, will ye? I can't see properly. It's getting dusky."

Mrs. Stitch popped her head in at the door and then went for the little brass lamp, which she placed near the window. She drew the shutters and then turned to her husband.

"I'm glad we don't live in the country," said she, with an important look on her face, as if she had news that would make Sam Stitch sit up and stare.

"The country's all right," replied Stitch, rubbing the thread in wax, and rethreading his needle. "It's all right in its place. Butter and eggs and cheese, you know. We can't do without them, nor can I do without Farmer Oats' breeches, with all this competition of four and twenty tailors."

"There's more things than butter and eggs in the country," said Mrs. Stitch, solemnly, with her hands on her hips, and her lips pursed out. "Folk are talking of a savage beastie that's roaming about. Mrs. Snips was telling me a queer tale, only tonight."

"Don't go by what Mrs. Snips says," snapped Mr. Stitch, crossly. "Snips is a poor sort of tailor. He can't even make a good buttonhole, much less seat a pair of trousers. As for making a new coat for the Alderman, he got that job by talking, not by sewing. He'll be the laughing stock of the town before long, you mark my words!" He bit his thread angrily, and turned to his work.

"Mrs. Snips was saying," continued Mrs. Stitch, without taking any notice of her husband's outburst, "Mrs. Snips was saying that there's a queer savage beastie been seen in Hollow Wood."

"Ah!" grunted Stitch. "Tell that to the marines, not to a respectable tailor. What does it matter to us? Let it stay there. Hollow Wood is far enough away."

"It would matter to us if the creature ate one of our children," said Mrs. Stitch severely.

"Why should it eat one of our children any more than a country child?"

"The country children will soon be finished, Mr. Stitch, for there aren't many of them. Then it will come here for *our* children!"

74

"Why should it eat our children any more than Snips's or Tack's or Patch's children? There are plenty of tailors in this town to supply children and not be missed," he went on, rather bitterly for such a kind-hearted man, but the memory of the Alderman's coat had upset him.

"I hope our children are better-looking than those Snips and Tack and Patch children," protested Mrs. Stitch haughtily. "I'll go and get your supper, Stitch. That beastie won't touch any of those wizened babies whilst our fat little chickabiddies are about."

She went out in a temper, and bustled about in the kitchen, clattering pans and shooing the cat from the hearth. Soon there was the smell of frying eggs, frizzling ham, and roasting coffee, and all the rosy Stitch children came running in from play.

"Mother! Mother!" they cried. "There's a monstrous animal in yonder wood. Tommy Snips has seen it and it has fierce eyes, sending out fire, and a long neck, and a great curving body, and no legs and a pair of horns on its head!"

"Did it roar at him?" asked Mr. Stitch with sarcasm.

"It let out a terrible hoot," shouted the children, excitedly, "but he didn't stop, he ran home as fast as he could."

"You stay here by the fireside, my dears," said Mrs. Stitch, "and don't venture out."

"Suppose it is a dragon," cried the eldest Stitch girl, who was in the top class at school. "Suppose it is a dragon, and it's waiting for a maiden to devour. Suppose I've to sit chained to a rock and wait for it to eat me!"

"It won't eat you if you stay indoors," exclaimed Mrs. Stitch, as she plumped the food on the table and drew up the chairs. "Oh, Stitch! Why don't you *do* something? You sit there, as calm as calm, and you don't care a bit."

"Do you expect me to go out and fight your wild beast?" asked Mr. Stitch indignantly, eating his ham and eggs.

That night the little Stitches went to bed with nightlights, and Mrs. Stitch fastened all the shutters herself, and bolted and barred the doors. All through the night she shivered and shook and talked to her unbelieving husband about the monster out in the woods across the river. Those woods were big enough to shelter an army of dragons. Stitch snored and heard not a word.

Next morning a tailor brought news of a white glistening trail he had seen, and the children were kept away from school. Doors were locked, the streets were quiet, and faces peered from windows looking at the few venturesome ones who dared to walk about.

There was a meeting of the tailors, but Mr. Stitch wouldn't go. He was too busy sewing Farmer Oats' breeches, he said.

"We must do something to make our country safe for the generations to come," proclaimed Mr. Snips, who was chairman. "We must make our town fit to live in, so that the smallest child can walk to school without fear."

"Hear! Hear!" cried little Mr. Button. "We must organize an army to fight this terrible dragon. Let it not be said we were cowards like Mr. Stitch when danger approached our beloved ones."

"We must go forth ourselves and slay the fierce beastie. Are we not renowned tailors who fear nothing?" cried Mr. Patch, and all the tailors cheered. Hurrah! Hurrah!

They went home singing through the streets to say good-bye to their wives and children whom they might never see again. They armed themselves with their biggest cutting-out scissors, their shears, their sharpest needles, their longest pins, their stilettos and bodkins. Mrs. Snips made a flag of patchwork, and gave it to her husband who was in charge of the little army. Then they clasped their wives to their breasts, kissed their children, and marched out of the town, the four and twenty tailors, four abreast. Only Stitch was left behind.

"It's all imagination," said he. "Moonshine! An old woman's tale! I've my work to do, and not much time to do it." He stitched away at Farmer Oats' breeches and finished them off.

Out of the town went the tailors, the little men who had never been in the country before. Across the river, down the lanes, they walked, among bluebells and red campions, between hedges where wrens and blackbirds sang, to the woods where the cuckoo called. As they went they brandished their little weapons fiercely and cheered one another on.

They walked up the hill, climbing among oak and fir and beech trees, startling the rabbits with their cries. At last they came near the spot where Tommy Snips had seen the wild beastie. There lay the bare rock behind which it lurked; its den must be near, and the fight would begin at any moment. They tightened their belts, and marched up to the rock.

"Saint George for Merry England," cried Snips, waving the patchwork flag, and they all cheered and waved their weapons. There was the beastie, lying on the rock, fast asleep with its house on its back! Mr. Patch raised his bodkin to stab; Mr. Snips felt the point of his long pin and prepared to throw it like a javelin; Mr. Button held his scissors ready. At that moment the snail awoke, and put out a pair of tiny horns with knobs at the ends, waving these inquiringly up and down.

" 'Tis like a Kyloe cow!" cried Mr. Snips in terror, and he turned round to flee. "Run, tailors, run," he shouted, and down the hill they tumbled, rolling over one another, dropping their pins and needles in the bracken, leaving their thimbles and scissors in the ferns.

"It's only a snail," said Dick Oats, who was minding the swine close by. "It's only a tiddley little snail!" He took it up in his fingers and moved it back to a cool piece of rock. "Won't my father laugh when I tell him! I'm glad Mr. Stitch wasn't there! All the tailors in the town except Stitch to fight a snail!"

How the rest of the people laughed, and the country folk most of all! One of them, who called himself a poet, made a rhyme about it, and sang it in the streets. This is how it went:

" *Four and twenty tailors went to fight a snail,*
The best man among them durst not touch her tail!
She put out her horns like a little Kyloe cow.
Run, tailors, run, or she'll get you all ere now!"

78

But the Alderman decided that Stitch was the best man to make his new coat, for he was the only one who stuck to his work, and took no notice of gossip and rumour.

Sing a Song of Sixpence

It was spring, and little catkins hung from the silver-birch, red tassels starred the larch-trees, and crimson tails dropped from the tall poplars. The King's garden had only a few flowers, tulips, primulas and daffadowndillies, but in the fields round the cottage where His Majesty lived, the cowslips and violets were out. Young calves and lambs frisked in the sweet grass, and the grey mare looked over the hawthorn hedge which separated the King's domain from the rest of the world. She nibbled a juicy morsel, and kept her soft eyes fixed on Peter, who was sowing a row of peas.

"Gerr up, Duchess!" scolded the gardener. "I can see ye. Be off! Don't be eating His Majesty's rose-trees." Duchess whinnied and stretched out her neck for another bite.

"Leave her alone, Peter." A voice came from the seat under the yew-arbour, and the King stepped out, with a poetry book under his arm.

"Beg pardon, sir. I didn't know you was there," said Peter, touching his cap.

"Yes, Peter. I am always somewhere, you know. You can't get away from me in this little kingdom of mine." He walked over to the hedge and rubbed Duchess's nose.

"Summer is a-cumin' in, Peter."

"Yes, Your Majesty, summer's a-comin' I suppose."

"Then we shall have roses and lilies, green peas and new potatoes, strawberries and cherries," said the King, looking round his garden at the bushes and plants, and the little green shoots.

"Yes, Your Majesty, if the birds don't take them," replied Peter, but the King didn't hear.

"This simple life is very refreshing, Peter. Sunshine and moonshine free. Not a care in the world, except the trivial lack of money. Parliament votes me little. However I can give you something I have saved for your faithfulness, Peter."

He put his hand in his pocket and brought out a lean purse. From it he took a sixpence.

"Don't mention it to the Queen, Peter. It's a little present from me to you."

Peter thanked the King, took the sixpence in his dirty hand, looked at the portrait of his master on its side, and put it in his corduroys. Then the King took Duchess by her forelock and led her gently away from the rose-trees, and Peter knelt down to cotton his peas, and to hang little paper flags over them to scare away the birds.

"The only flags our King will have," said he to himself, "but he doesn't mind."

Peter was the coachman as well as the gardener. He groomed the grey mare, and plaited her tail with yellow straws and blue ribbons on Sundays when the King drove to the village church. He waited on his royal master, too, and curled his wig and cleaned his boots. His wife, Nancy, was the dairymaid, cook and laundrymaid all in one.

The King and Queen had only these two servants, but they were a contented royal couple, whose wants were few. That was a golden age, when every man was his own master, and all were equal.

"My dear!" exclaimed the King, as he looked through the parlour window a few days later. "How lovely the cherry-blossom is! What a fine lot of cherries we shall have!"

The Queen put down her mending and came to his side. The cherry-trees were a foam of white blossom, the dark branches were covered with clusters of bloom, like snowballs perched on the trees. From one smooth trunk to another hung a clothes-line, with the royal washing drying in the sunshine, fluttering white as the flowers above. Blackbirds, tomtits, and chaffinches flew up and down, and petals of the sweet flowers dropped like melting snow to the ground.

"Yes, there's plenty of blossom," agreed the Queen. "We ought to have a good crop, if Peter Gardener keeps down the blackbirds. You know, my dear, there are too many birds in our garden."

"Tut! Tut!" cried the King. "They are my only subjects nowadays. Nobody remembers me but the birds. They are my jesters. They whistle and sing, and amuse me with their antics." He pointed to a tomtit upside down on a bough. Then he grunted, rather crossly: "I do wish, my own, that Nancy wouldn't always hang my nightshirt in front of the parlour window. Why is it always washing day?"

"Nancy likes to keep your clothes in the royal manner, my love," explained the Queen; "white as the snow." She took up her needle, and went on with the patch she was putting on a sheet.

Spring turned slowly into summer; bluebells came and went, leaving an army of faded stalks; cuckoos called "Cuckoo! Cuckoo!" from the ash-tree in the big field over the garden hedge, and away they flew over the cottage to the larch-wood, where the tiny green cones now grew. Swallows built their nests in the eaves of the thatched roof, and darted with tails open like fans and backs gleaming like blue silk. Thrushes and blackbirds laid their precious jewels of eggs in the thorn hedge round the garden, and a robin flew in at the ever-open window of the King's bedroom, and made its nest in the gold crown which lay unheeded on the oak chest in the corner of the room.

"Don't disturb it," said the King to Nancy who wanted to clear away the mess. "I won't wear my crown till the eggs are hatched. There's plenty of time."

"His Majesty will put up with any inconvenience," said Nancy, when she reported the nest to Peter.

The roses were blooming in the garden, and the young robins were learning to fly from their golden home, when the cherries were ripe. The King and Queen went out to visit the row of beehives, which stood among the flowers, and for a few minutes they watched the bees. The Queen stooped to pick the blue irises and cat-mint which bordered the bee-garden but the King stood on tiptoes and drew down a branch of a cherry-tree. He picked a bunch and said to the Queen:

> "*Open your mouth and shut your eyes,*
> *And you shall have a fine surprise.*"

84

So she shut her eyes tightly, and opened her round mouth, and waited, whilst he popped in the cherries.

"Delicious!" she laughed. "I must make some cherry-jam."

"Could we have a cherry-pie, tomorrow, my dear? We have had rice pudding for months, and it's my birthday, you know."

"Certainly," replied the Queen, and she went to the kitchen to talk to Nancy.

"His Majesty would like a cherry-pie for his birthday dinner, tomorrow, Nancy," said she.

"Yes, ma'am. I'll tell Peter to pick a basketful before them plaguey blackbirds get holt of 'em."

But Peter Gardener forgot, and the next day when Nancy came running from her kitchen door, there was never a cherry on the trees. Not one was left, and there, on the hedge, perched a row of cheeky birds, flirting their tails and cocking their heads at her.

"My word! You are a naughty crew," grumbled Nancy. "I'll tell the King, that I will, and he'll cut all your heads off." The blackbirds chuckled with delight, and Nancy waddled off to the King.

"There ain't *one* cherry left, Your Majesty," said she, poking her head in at the parlour door where the King and Queen sat at breakfast. "It's all those blackbirds. I told you what it would be like, Your Majesty. Shall Peter destroy them all?"

"Oh dear," sighed the King, "I *did* want a cherry-pie. There's something romantic about a cherry,— all those little red fellows nestled under a white pie crust. Isn't there a poem about a cherry, my dear?"

He thought a moment, and Nancy twiddled her hands in her apron, impatiently.

"Yes, this is it:

> *"A riddle-me, riddle-me, rot, tot-tot*
> *A little wee man in a little red coat.*
> *A stick in his hand, and a stone in his throat,*
> *If you answer this riddle I'll give you a groat."*

"A cherry," said the Queen, quickly, and the King went to his counting-house to fetch a groat for her.

Nancy fidgeted. "Is that all, Your Majesty? Shall Peter sweep away those blackytops?"

"Certainly not!" cried the King, and Nancy hurried out to talk to Peter.

"Peter," said she. "Something must be done. There'll be no fruit in the garden."

"I'd shoot the pests, but the King loves them," answered Peter, dolefully.

"There's no reason why we shouldn't teach 'em a lesson," said Nancy. "Have you got that sixpence the King gave you once on a time, Peter?" Peter nodded and he reached for the holly-wood money-box which stood on the kitchen mantelpiece. Nancy whispered some advice to him, and he whispered back.

"Thou art a clever wench, Nancy," said he.

He went to a neighbouring farm and spent his sixpence on a pocketful of rye. This he sprinkled on the garden path under the cherry-trees, and tilted a large riddle over it. When the crowd of blackbirds was safely underneath, eating the delicious fare, he pulled the string, and caught them all.

"Hist," said he to the fluttering scolding mob. "I'm not going to harm ye. Be quiet, will ye?"

He carried them into the kitchen, where Nancy had made an enormous empty pie.

She held up the crust, and into the space Peter pushed the protesting birds. Nancy popped the lid back on them, and they sorted themselves out, and stood in an orderly fashion, twenty-four of them, waiting quietly to see what would happen.

"I'll larn 'em," muttered Nancy. "I'll larn 'em to take the King's cherries," and the blackbirds bent their heads in sorrow for their misdeeds.

The King and Queen sat down to dinner, and Peter, in his white apron, brought in the lordly dish, whilst Nancy peeped through the door, a wide grin on her homely face.

"What have we here?" asked the King, but the Queen shook her head. "It must be a surprise of Nancy's," said she.

The King cut a slit in the pie-crust, and twenty-four blackbirds poked out their round heads, and from twenty-four beaks came a twitter. The birds flew out on to the tablecloth, and there, in front of the King, they sang their sweetest song.

"Excellent!" cried the King. "A delightful surprise; a dainty dish to set before me," and the Queen clasped her hands in joy.

"If we did not live in the Golden Age, I would knight you, Peter. As it is you shall be promoted to the post of head gardener."

"Thank you, Your Majesty," said Peter politely. "But I am already head gardener," he said to himself.

Through the open window went the birds when

their song of thanksgiving was done, back to the hedge where they chatted noisily, and vowed they'd never take another cherry.

"Now bring in the bread and cheese," said the King.

When the meal was finished, the King went to his counting-house and took out his moneybags. He spread his silver on the table and counted it. Ten, twelve, twenty, thirty sixpences. Could he spare a sixpence for Peter who had provided that musical treat? Could he afford it? He tinkled the bell and Peter came in.

"Here's a little present for you, Peter," said he. "Keep it in your moneybox. The blackbirds' song was divine."

"Thank you, sire," said Peter, politely, and he bowed himself out. He put the jolly sixpence in the holly-wood box and rattled it to hear the sound of riches.

The Queen sat in her parlour. A pie full of singing birds was all very well for a poet like the King, bread and cheese was good enough for Peter, but she wanted more dainty fare. She opened the corner cupboard and took out a honeycomb. From her pocket she brought a piece of bread. She had scarcely begun her feast when there came a shriek from the garden. The King dropped his sixpences, and the Queen left her honey, and they both ran to see what was the matter.

There, by the clothes-line under the cherry-trees, stood unhappy Nancy with her hand to her face. Over the rosebuds flew a blackbird and in his beak was poor Nancy's little snub nose.

"Drop it! Drop it," shouted Peter, chasing after, but away went the bird to the wood.

"That settles it!" cried Peter. "Your Majesty, I must buy a clacker this very day, and scare those cheeky birds away, or they might take the royal nose."

He put his arm round Nancy, and together they sat under the flapping clothes, bewailing the missing nose.

"What a day of adventure is my birthday!" exclaimed the King. "I must write a poem to celebrate the events."

He took a new quill pen and sat down at his writing-table, and this is the song which he wrote for the Queen to sing:

> "Sing a song of sixpence,
> A pocket full of rye,
> Four and twenty blackbirds,
> Baked in a pie.
> When the pie was opened,
> The birds began to sing.
> Wasn't that a dainty dish
> To set before the King?
> The King was in his counting-house,
> Counting out his money,
> The Queen was in the parlour,
> Eating bread and honey,
> The maid was in the garden,
> Hanging out the clothes,
> When by came a blackbird
> And snapped off her nose!"

"Look!" cried the Queen, who was leaning through the window. "Here comes Nancy with her nose again!"

"There came a Jenny Wren, and popped it on again," said Nancy, curtseying. "I'm quite well now, Your Majesty."

So the King dipped his quill into the ink and added an end to the song.

> *"Then came by a Jenny Wren,*
> *And she popped it on again."*

Peter, Peter

Once upon a time there lived a little man named Peter Piper. He was not the Peter Piper who picked a peck of peppercorns, but quite another Peter, for he was so small he would be lost in a peck measure.

He had a wife as little as himself. She had only one fault—she was always hungry! However much she had to eat, she wanted more!

"More rice pudding! More bread and milk! More sago, and tapioca, and barley kernels! More porridge!" she cried, beating her spoon on the table, and little Peter ran out of the house in despair.

He gleaned in the cornfields for wheat to make her bread, and he carried his load home on his little bent back. He hunted in the woods for nuts and blackberries for her dessert, and filled his small brown sack and his pannikin to the brim. He climbed the crabapple trees for green crabs, and the sloe-bushes for black sloes, and gathered the hips and haws from the hedgerows, just as if he were a bird, or a squirrel, or some wild creature. Indeed, he looked like a tiny wild man of the woods, in his green hat with a jay's feather, his brown leather trousers, and his rag of a shirt which fluttered about his bare brown arms.

All the creatures of the countryside knew Peter, and they all offered him advice about his little wife who was so hungry.

"Feed her on worms," said the robin. "She won't ask for more, but if she does there are plenty in the rich earth."

"Feed her on rabbits," said the foxes. "There are so many young rabbits running about in the fields, they will satisfy her hunger."

"Oh no!" cried the rabbits, when they heard. "Give her grass. Don't give her us, please Peter Piper. Give her green grass, there is grass for everyone."

"I don't think she likes such things," sighed poor Peter. "It's very trying, for I do want to make her happy."

"Give her milk," said the cows, and Peter filled his little can. But Mrs. Peter drank it up in a moment and asked for more, and when Peter got back to the field the cows had gone to the farmyard.

At last he said to his wife: "My dear, I don't know what to do! The fields and woods can't provide for you. We must leave our little house and move to the town, where I hear there is lots of food. There are grocers' shops and bakeries and bun shops and milk shops. Surely we shall get enough for you to eat there."

Mrs. Peter was delighted, and she packed up her tiny belongings in a brown paper parcel, and followed her little husband along the lanes and roads to the great town.

They were rather frightened at first; they were so small and the people were so big. They crept along the shadows of the walls and dodged about between the long legs which seemed to fill the pavements.

Then they came to a greengrocer's shop.

"This looks like home," whispered Peter, and Mrs. Peter nodded.

"Let us live here," said she, happily. "Look at the apples, Peter, and the cabbages and oranges and turnips! It was worth coming all that long way, wasn't it?" and Peter agreed.

They glided silently through the doorway and sat down in a dark corner behind a pile of cabbages, waiting until the shop was quiet and the customers had gone. At last, when the shutters were up and the shop was locked for the night, Mrs. Peter unpacked her little kettle and frying-pan and made herself at home.

Such a feast there was! Oranges and nuts, apples and bananas, potatoes fried and cabbage boiled, carrots stewed and onions braised! Mrs. Peter really got enough to eat that night, but in the morning, when the greengrocer came to unlock his shop, there was a terrible bother.

"Who's been here? Who's been eating *my* stores?" he roared, like the bear in the fairy tale. Mrs. Peter trembled so much she made the cabbage leaves quiver and the greengrocer hauled out the tiny couple and shook them.

"My goodness me! So it's you, is it?" he shouted, and his voice nearly deafened poor Mrs. Peter, for her ears were like little shells. "Who would have believed it! Out you go!"

He tossed them into the street as if they had been a couple of bad apples, and shut the door against them.

"Oh, deary-deary-me!" sobbed poor little Mrs. Peter. "I've lost my frying-pan, Peter."

"Never mind, dear. We'll get another," said Peter comfortingly, and he took her small hand and sidled along the pavement with her.

Soon they came to a baker's shop, so they stepped across the door-sill and hid among the bread. That was a warm soft bed for the two wanderers and they fell asleep, tired out after their adventure. All day they slept and it wasn't till night came and the baker had gone home that they rubbed their eyes and sat up.

Mrs. Peter sat on a currant bun and Peter fed her. Cakes and doughnuts, sugar-buns, vanilla-slices! All disappeared before the hungry little Mrs. Peter was satisfied. But when morning came and they had just swept up the crumbs, and tidied the shop, there was a terrible to-do!

"Who's been here? Who's been eating *my* cakes?" bellowed the baker. Mrs. Peter trembled so much that a coconut rock fell to the floor and the baker found the culprits.

"It's you, is it? What do you mean by eating my buns? Out you go!"

He threw them both into the street as if they had been two crusts of bread, and banged the door behind them.

"Oh, deary-deary-deary-me!" groaned Mrs. Peter. "I've lost my kettle, Peter."

"Never mind, darling. We'll get another," said Peter, and he took her arm and led her along the path.

They walked and they walked till they came to a dairy; then they crept through the door and hid among the milkcans. Mrs. Peter tried to make a little home in the corner, and Peter found a pocket

of hay in which she could lie. She spread out her tiny handkerchief and put her little tin mug and plate in the middle.

At night, when the shop was quiet, Peter fed her. Milk and cream and eggs! Such a hungry little Mrs. Peter sat there, eating and drinking all night. Then, as usual, they both swept up the shop with the heather brush they had brought with them, and left all tidy.

When the milkman came, he held up his hands in amazement.

"Who's been here? There's only one person who could eat and drink all this, and it's Mrs. Peter Piper."

He hunted in the pocket of hay and brought out the little frightened pair.

Instead of scolding them, he laughed and laughed.

"My old father, away in the country, knows all about you," said he. "He's told me, too. I'll send you to him. He wants a tidy, hard-working little fellow like Peter to help him, and he will give Mrs. Peter a home, too." He laughed again and went out for his horse and cart.

Soon they were all journeying away to the country again, to the farm where the dairyman's father lived, and Mrs. Peter and Peter sat on the seat dangling their legs and whispering about their new home.

Can you guess where it was? Do you know?

In the garden was an enormous pumpkin, and Mrs. Peter made her little house within it! It was so large she had food all round her and as it grew every day there was always plenty for her to eat.

As for Peter, he swept the barns and fed the chickens and gathered the eggs and looked for mushrooms and played with the little grandchildren who lived at the farm.

Sometimes he sang a little song about himself, and his wife looked out from the pumpkin window and smiled down at him when she heard the words.

> *Peter, Peter, Pumpkin-eater,*
> *Had a wife, and couldn't keep her.*
> *He put her in a pumpkin shell,*
> *And there he kept her very well.*

"I *am* very well, Peter," she called. "I never want to move again. This pumpkin is the nicest little house in all the world," and Peter waved his little green hat with the jay's feather and went on with his sweeping.

Johnny at the Fair

Johnny Green was courting Jenny Daw. Every Sunday they walked up the fields together, and they sat on a stile, and talked of the future. Johnny cut a stick and Jenny gathered some flowers, and they went back to the farm, for Johnny was cowman and Jenny was dairymaid.

They had seen a cottage where they would live when they were wed, near enough for Johnny to get to the cows at dawn. They planned what they would have in it—rush-bottomed chairs, and a horse-hair sofa, and a pair of brass candlesticks, and a copper warming-pan.

"And we'll have a garden full of flowers," said Jenny. "I love flowers as much as I love you."

Then came the day of the Fair. Johnny had permission to go to it, to buy things for the wedding. There would be many useful things for sale at the Fair.

"And I want a basket of beautiful flowers, Johnny, the nicest in the Fair, and garlands, too," said Jenny. "But I want a bunch of blue ribbons more than anything."

"Whatever do you want ribbons for, Jenny?" asked Johnny. "You are pretty enough without ribbons."

"To tie up my bonny brown hair," laughed Jenny, giving him a kiss, and away he went, smiling and waving his stick, whistling down the lane to the highroad.

It was many miles to the Fair, but Johnny was lucky, for he hadn't gone far along the turnpike, when a cart overtook him and a man leaned over the side.

"Want a lift?" he asked. "Going to the Fair?" Johnny nodded, and jumped in thankfully. Everyone gave a walker a lift in those days, for it was counted prideful and wrong to pass a poor fellow trudging along the road. They picked up other people on the way, and soon there were four of them sitting in the cart, a merry company, who told their names and trades and talked of the glories of the Fair to which they were going.

When they arrived they all thanked the driver, and wished each other luck before they parted company. Johnny was there in good time, but the fairground was already crowded. He elbowed his way among the countrymen, with his eyes agog at the number of sideshows and the fun around him.

If only Jenny had been with him! The music of the dobby-horses, the clatter of the soaring swingboats, the sharp reports at the shooting-booth, mingled with the cries of the cheapjacks, pulled Johnny here and there to see what was going on.

He found his way to the cattle-market, and watched the cows and calves being sold, and guessed the weights of sheep, and poked fat pigs in their sides. He talked to men who had brought horses to show, and admired the great mares and foals.

Next he came to a cheapjack selling yellow necklaces.

"Come along, young man," he called when he saw Johnny's rosy face. "Here's something for your sweetheart. Here's your chance. A gold necklace for a shilling."

"Well, it *looks* like gold," said Johnny, "but how did you know about Jenny?" He bought the necklace and went on. He had always wanted to see Jenny in a gold chain like the quality.

He came to a man selling herb pills that would cure all things. "The cure-all!" he shouted. "It will cure every ill from broken hearts to chilblains! A shilling a box and worth a guinea!"

"Now young man," he called when he saw Johnny's cheerful face. "Let me sell you a box. You can give it to your sweetheart, and she'll thank you for the rest of your life, for 'she will never be ill, if she takes my pill'. A guinea for a shilling."

Johnny took out a shilling and bought a box of the wonderful pills.

He went on to the flower-stalls. There were bright red geraniums and purple pansies, but Johnny was looking for something else.

"Buy a flower for your sweetheart, sir," wheedled the woman. "Here's a rose-tree. Roses bring luck. Or a lily. Every lass loves a lily. Buy a flower for your lady, sir."

From the roof of the stall hung garlands, woven wreaths of flowers which pretty girls wore around their necks, like lovely scented necklaces. There were wreaths of pinks and columbines and marigolds, entwined with green leaves. Johnny pointed to a wreath of lilies-of-the-valley, a delicate white garland, with the hundred bells tinkling in their dark green leaves.

"That's the wreath for my Jenny," said he, and the woman lifted it down with careful caressing hands.

Near it was a garland of roses, little red moss-roses, each flower half hidden in its nest of mossy fronds, and tiny white roses, with golden stamens in the centre.

"That wreath, too," said Johnny. " It will just suit my Jenny. She is very partial to roses."

Then he chose a basketful of pretty flowers, picking here and there, bachelor's-buttons, goldylocks, love-lies-bleeding, Star-of-Bethlehem, all the favourite old flowers.

He paid for them all, and carried them off, but the very next stall brought him to a standstill again.

On it were birds, cages and cages of birds for sale. Canaries and greenfinches, and jolly bullfinches. Johnny wanted no "bullies", there were too many of them in the garden at home, eating the cherries, but he wanted to look at the little twittering crea-tures.

He could scarcely get near, for children dragged at their parents and cried, "Buy one! Oh! Buy one!" and wives whispered to husbands, and husbands put their hands deep into their pockets to find the precious money hidden away from pickpockets.

"Johnny? Johnny?" called a queer voice, and Johnny turned quickly to meet the eyes of a red and grey parrot.

"If only I could buy it," said Johnny, "but it would take the best part of my wages. Fancy knowing my name and saying it so human-like!" The stall-holder said it was strange, but his own name was Johnny, too, and wouldn't Johnny like to bu him?

"I'll have a singing canary," said Johnny. "I couldn't carry the poll home, even if I did buy him." So a canary it was, a fine little cock, which sang and chirruped, until it was wrapped up in paper and tucked under Johnny's other arm.

He saw a gingerbread stall, with the cleverest things all made out of gingerbread. There was a castle at the back, with turrets and drawbridge, and a row of gingerbread soldiers walking near. Only a penny for a gingerbread soldier! There were men and women, too, the women in bonnets, the men with currant buttons down their suits. Johnny filled his left-hand pocket with some and walked to the next stall where sweets of every kind were strewn.

He bought twisty barley-sugar, and little pink and white lozenges with "I love you" and "You are a dear" printed upon them. They would make Jenny laugh! He bought a stick of curled black liquorice, and a basket of lemon-kali, and treacle toffee, and aniseed balls. These he stuffed into his capacious right-hand pocket.

He tried his luck at a coconut-shy, and came away with two coconuts.

With his arms and pockets full he entered a tent. "Threepence to see the mouse queen," called the showman, as Johnny went in. There, on a table, were four little mice harnessed with silk bridles and belts. They drew a tiny carriage with red velvet cushions, and in the carriage sat a white mouse with blue spangled skirts.

"Fancy that now!" cried Johnny to his neighbour. "What would they do if our tabby came in!"

Next door was a juggler, who tossed six plates in the air at once, and a conjurer who brought a white rabbit out of Johnny's empty hat. Johnny spent so long looking at these wonders that it grew dark, and he thought of the journey home. But more marvels awaited him.

A man walked in stilts through the Fair, striding through the laughing people like a giant. A dwarf turned somersaults and rolled like a ball along a coloured carpet. A kilted man played a sad air on bagpipes—like the killing of pigs to Johnny's ear. A negro rattled a pair of bones and sang a black man's song.

Every one of these wanted some pennies, and Johnny's pockets got lighter and lighter till they were quite empty.

At last the showmen began to close their tents. The boothkeepers ate their supper of fish and chips. The dobby-horses went round for the last time. The negro, the Scotsman, and the dwarf sat on a bench together and divided their money. The birds were covered up and asleep.

Johnny hitched his canary under his coat to keep it warm, seized his garlands and coconuts and parcels, and looked up at the sky. Stars blazed in the high heavens. It was nearly midnight.

"I must be going home now," said he.

"Have you far to go?" asked one of the men.

Johnny told him, and he cried: "You'll be walking the stars out of the sky! You won't be home till cock crow."

Then it was that Johnny thought of the blue ribbons. "Why, I've forgotten the bunch of blue ribbons for my Jenny!" he exclaimed. But never a blue ribbon was left at the Fair.

"Blue ribbons?" echoed the stallkeeper. "We're sold out of all our ribbons. You should have thought of it earlier, my son."

So Johnny started on the weary journey home, along the soft white dusty roads, gleaming under the moon like white ribbons themselves. Rabbits scuttled across the path, sometimes an owl flew silently past. He heard the sound of horses cropping in the fields alongside and the barking of a dog far away. In the cage under his arm the canary fluttered its wings uneasily, wondering when the rocking of its little ship would cease. The garlands sent out waves of sweet scent, flooding Johnny's aching head with pleasure. The gingerbread men clung stickily together, banging against his side.

He crossed the river, he walked through villages, he strode through dewy fields and stumbled through dark woods, taking the narrow field-paths to make his journey shorter. At last he saw the farm in front of him. It was morning, and he would have to begin milking as soon as he had had a bite to eat. What would Jenny say to all he had to tell her? He'd forgotten her ribbon, and not brought one useful thing for the cottage!

As he walked up the path to the farmhouse, he heard a mournful little song coming from the attic window, and he stopped to listen to the words. This is what he heard:

> " *Oh dear! What can the matter be?*
> *Oh dear! What can the matter be?*
> *Oh dear! What can the matter be?*
> *Johnny's so long at the fair!*

He promised to buy me a basket of posies,
A garland of lilies, a garland of roses,
He promised to buy me a bunch of blue ribbons,
To tie up my bonny brown hair!"

"Here I am, Jenny," he called. "Better late than never." Then he sang in his turn:

" I've remembered to bring you a basket of posies,
A garland of lilies, a garland of roses,
I've forgotten to buy you a bunch of blue ribbons,
To tie up your bonny brown hair!"

So Jenny ran downstairs, and kindled the kitchen fire, and made Johnny a cup of tea, and he told her all I have told you, and more besides. As for the bunch of blue ribbons, he bought that the very next time he went to the market town, so it didn't matter so much after all.